ISBN: 978-1-63732-750-0

Real Shadows

M.E. Clayton

DEDICATION

For my son –
You'll never know just how much I love your laugh and pray you're happy.

CONTENTS

ACKNOWLEDGMENTS

The first acknowledgment will always be my husband. There aren't enough words to express my gratitude for having this man in my life. There is a little bit of him in every hero I dream up, and I can't thank God enough for bringing him into my life. Thirty years, and still going strong!

Second, there's my family; my daughter, my son, my grandchildren, my sister, and my mother. Family is everything, and I have one of the best. They are truly the best cheerleaders I could ever ask for, and I never forget just how truly blessed I am to have them in my life.

And, of course, there's Kamala. This woman is not only my beta and idea guinea pig, but she's also one of my closest friends. She's been with me from the beginning of this journey, and we're going to ride this thing to the end. Kam's the encouragement that sparked it all, folks.

And, finally, I'd like to thank everyone who's purchased, read, reviewed, shared, and supported me and my writing. Thank you so much for helping make this dream a reality and a happy, fun one at that! I cannot say thank you enough.

PROLOGUE

My many keys jingled endlessly as I unlocked my front door. My landlord hadn't uttered a word when I'd asked him if it was okay to call out a locksmith to install two additional deadbolts to my door when I had moved in. He had simply said that it was okay, had accepted the copy of the new keys, then had docked the cost from my second month's rent.

I've learned over the years that not all landlords were willing to let you alter their properties on your first day as a tenant. I'd lucked out with Richard, though. He hadn't objected, nor had he pried into why. Not in all the two years that I've lived here has he once asked me about my obsession with locks, and I was extremely grateful for his respect for privacy.

After the final lock was disengaged, I swung my front door open, then stepped inside. I dropped my purse on the light green sofa that took up most of the living room, then headed towards the kitchen with my bag of Mexican take-out.

I was only two steps past the sofa when my eyes caught sight of the silver ceramic bunny rabbit that lived on the second shelf of the bookcase that had come with the apartment, same as the light green sofa had.

The bag of take-out slipped out of my hand as I noticed how the little guy was now facing east instead of west.

Like he always was.

My heart started racing and my body fell under its routine paralysis. Fear—*real fear*—formed in the pit of my stomach, then branched out until it infused every cell in my body.

I couldn't process sound over the rush of blood in my ears and the frantic pulsing of my heart. My mind would not allow my eyes look left nor right. My mind did allow them to water, though. It allowed them to water, and silent tears began streaming down my face.

I stared at that silver ceramic bunny, and it was amazing how he could be a symbol for both safety and danger, all in one. He was a beacon for safety

1

when he was facing west, but he was a sign of danger when he was facing in any other direction. Even if he were still facing west, he could still be a sign of danger if you didn't pay enough attention to *how* he was facing west.

See, there was a reason he sat alone on that particular shelf; a shelf that was never dusted, a shelf that had superficial literature on it that I would never read. There was a reason why he faced west in a very specific manner.

Because I knew that *he* couldn't help himself.

Somehow, he knew all about my fixation with grey bunny rabbits. I had no idea how he knew, but he did. He had to have known the comfort they had brought me when I was younger. He had to have known about the stuffed bunny that I'd had for years. He had to have known because he's gifted me with the exact replica over the years. However, what he didn't know was why this particular silver ceramic bunny was important to me now. It was no longer a symbol of comfort but used as a warning system.

If that bunny was moved, even a fraction of a millimeter in any direction, I'd know that he found me again. I would know that he found me again, and that he'd been in my home.

Like he has now, once again.

If I got out of this moment alive, this would be the seventh time that I've had to move over a six-year span; the seventh time where I will have to try to find unknown shelter again, and an uneventful job to feed myself with.

So far, he's remained in the dark, opting to mentally torture me rather than outright attack me. It was almost as if he realized that, by attacking me, that would be the end to his game. If he came after me in the light, I'd be able to identify him, possibly fight him. However, I knew he didn't want that.

He wanted a victim.

More importantly, he wanted our sick, twisted, one-sided relationship to continue. He's been stalking me for six years, and every time that he's found me, the defeated punch to my chest felt just as painful as the ones before.

I just wanted a normal life.

I wanted a life without some creep determining my every move. I wanted a life where I had friends and a steady job that I could complain about.

I wanted a life where the police didn't look at me like I was crazy.

Ignoring the food on the floor, I walked over to the bookshelf, grabbed the silver bunny, then held on to it until I could function enough to start packing up my life again.

CHAPTER 1

Fallon ~

Most people would balk at driving across the country with their life savings in a suitcase, but desperation overshadowed common sense at this point.

Fleeing California-which was exactly what I was doing-with everything I had seemed like a sound decision at the time. Plus, even if I did end up getting robbed at gunpoint, well, there were worse things that could happen to a person, and that thought, in itself, was as grim as it got.

As self-centered creatures, we always think that our worries and woes were the worst out there. However, if given the choice, I'd rather get robbed than raped. I'd rather get robbed than murdered. I'd rather get robbed than lose a child. I'd rather get robbed than live in constant fear of a threat I couldn't identify.

Hence, why I was fleeing California and heading towards North Dakota.

Why North Dakota, you ask?

Because no one lived in goddamn North Dakota.

Well, that wasn't entirely true.

Lots of people lived in North Dakota, but they lived in the 'big' towns of Fargo and Grand Forks. My destination was a little nowhere town called Brant. Imagine any small town surrounded by farmlands with only one high school, maybe two grocery stores, and one auto shop that could charge you an arm and leg but didn't because the owner was your baseball coach.

That was Brant, North Dakota.

Ideally, it wasn't a place you wanted to move to if your goal was to be invisible, but I've been trying that method for over six years, and it hasn't worked for me. After calling my landlord to give him my thirty-day notice, calling all necessary utility companies, packing my few belongings, then withdrawing every cent I had from the bank, I had purchased a burner phone, called the only person in the world that I still kept in contact with, then headed towards North Dakota.

3

I'd grown up in foster care after losing my parents when I was seven. While it had been rough to lose my parents the way I had, foster care hadn't been as horrible as it could have been. Oh, I was familiar with neglect and abuse, but I had never endured anything that I couldn't come back from.

I'd been a shy child, and the fact that I'd been scrawny hadn't helped me much. I'd been easily picked on and bullied, but I had thought of it more as picking my battles, rather than bowing down. Besides, every kid in foster care had been doing the same thing that I'd been doing; we all had just been trying to survive.

My dreams of being adopted by a loving family had been dashed early on, and like most foster kids, I'd grown up quickly after that. I might have still been picked on, but I'd been independent, depending on no one, since I was around eleven-years-old. Once the reality of life had slapped me across the face, my singular focus had been to make sure that I'd had a plan when I fostered out of care. The hopping around from home to home hadn't bothered me so much as it had saddened me constantly. No matter how many times I tried to fight against the feeling of rejection, it had always hit me hard.

There'd been a couple of homes that had wanted to keep me, but without outright adopting me, they couldn't because foster care was all about supply and demand. They shuffled kids around like pawns on a chessboard, making room for the newly deserted or rejected.

No longer wanting to be at the mercy of anyone, I had started working after school as soon as I'd been old enough. Little had I known that life choice would make me a perfect candidate to reside in the orphanage instead of an actual home. Homes were for the children still in need; the babies, the helpless, the mentally challenged. They were the ones who needed loving care. The fifteen-years-olds, the ones who could work and go to school themselves, hadn't required such things as love and guidance.

I had spent the last three years in foster care going to school and working my ass off with part-time after-school jobs. I had wanted to work, but I'd also known that I needed my high school diploma more if I were ever going to amount to anything in my life.

During those younger years, the only thing I'd had of any sentimental value had been a ratted, torn, grey bunny rabbit that had either been given to me on my first day in foster care, or had been a toy from the time in my life where I'd had a family; a time before my parents had been killed by a drunk driver.

That rabbit had been named Silver, and he had withstood years and years of house shuffling, bullying, neglect, and abuse. I had held on to that piece of…consistency all my life, but then he had come up missing when I'd just turned sixteen-years-old. I could remember tearing up the entire orphanage looking for him, but I never did find him. Everyone I had asked about him had claimed not to have known what happened to him.

However, one of them had lied.

Still, I wouldn't know that until six years later, when I had walked into my one-bedroom apartment after working the closing shift as a bartender at Drink This, a local college bar in northern California. I hadn't been able to swing college, no matter how good my grades had been, so I'd opted for being happy to just be able to hold down a good job that could support me without the need for government assistance.

I'd never been proud, but I'd wanted more in life than what foster care had shown me. However, I'll never forget walking into my apartment, then heading towards my bedroom, only to see the grey, worn, stuffed bunny rabbit sitting proudly in the middle of my bed.

For months before the rabbit had appeared on my bed, I'd thought my mind was playing tricks on me. I thought I'd been under adult-life stress or something. I'd come home to small items being misplaced or slightly skewed in one way or another. It had been small things that had made me think, *oh, hey, I must have forgotten to put it back.*

It had never been anything huge or obvious. There were times that I'd get in my car and the seat was slightly pushed back or a window rolled down; stuff like that. It had all been minor incidences that could easily be explained away by carelessness or just not thinking. It had never occurred to me that it might be something more sinister until I'd seen that rabbit on my bed.

My rabbit.

The shock of seeing it had rendered me immobile for a few incomprehensive minutes before I'd done what we all yelled at the stupid girl in the movie for. Instead of calling the police and making sure I hadn't touched anything, I had snapped out of my shock, walked towards my bed, then had picked up the rabbit to verify if it was, indeed, the one from my childhood.

Holding the rabbit in my hand had brought on real feelings of fright and violation. Never having had experienced anything like a stalker before, the knowledge that this hadn't just any old stalker, but someone from my past and was still fixated on me all these years later, had been numbing.

And like every time since then, I had called the police. And while they had taken my fright seriously, they hadn't taken the crime seriously. I'd gotten a whole bunch of nothing from them. They had taken the rabbit as 'evidence' but had politely reminded me that there was nothing they could do without proof of something more.

I had remained in that apartment for two more months before the paranoia had pushed me to the edge of insanity. I had moved to another town, and I've been moving to new towns every time he's found me. Or, hell, it could be a she for all I knew.

Over the years, some officers have been compassionate, and some have been assholes. An invisible stalker was not high on their priority list, and I got it.

I really did.

This was a personal crime that only affected me and, so far, I hadn't been harmed physically. Police officers had real crime they had to deal with every day. There were murders, rapes, robberies, and shootings they had to deal with. My random intruder-who liked to misplace my ceramic rabbit-was hardly a national tragedy.

Still, my fear? That'd been real.

It still was.

I'd done everything short of changing my name to escape this…person. I've changed so many jobs and cities and appearances over the years that I no longer knew what there was left to do. So, I'd called the only person that I could remotely consider a friend, Karla Craig, and had told her everything. She was the only person I considered a friend because I never stayed in a place long enough to make friends. I had kept to myself out of fear. I also hadn't been ready to explain my crazy to anyone because that's how I felt sometimes.

I felt crazy.

Karla and I had grown up in foster care together, but when she was around sixteen, she'd been claimed by a long-lost relative, and he'd taken her to live with him and his family. I'd been happy for her but devastated by the loss. Friends-*true friends*-were hard to come by in foster care. Though we had stayed in touch, our lives were definitely polar opposites.

After telling Karla everything, she had insisted that I move to North Dakota and start fresh. Talking with her, she made living in Small Town, USA sound so wonderful and safe. She had also pointed out that it was a far cry from California, and where a stranger wouldn't stand out in the busy streets of California, a stranger would definitely stand out in Brant, North Dakota.

So, I had packed up everything I owned, pulled out every cent I had in the bank, filled up my gas tank, then had taken off the next day after taking care of my work, rental, and utilities obligations.

And now, driving through the great state of Montana, I was almost to my destination, and hopefully new life.

A life where I didn't fear every shadow.

CHAPTER 2

Xander ~

North Dakota in July could be just as warm as Florida. The sweat dripping down my face and back could attest to that.

Still, I loved it.

The winters in North Dakota didn't leave much room for outdoor work or activities, so during the warmer months, I relished in the physical activity that working construction brought on. Yeah, technically, I was a contractor and the owner of the company, but that didn't mean I had let the titles turn me into being lazy and out of touch with the manual labor side of things. I still loved working with my hands, no matter how many hours I spent behind a desk.

Eight years ago, I'd only been twenty-two-years-old when a horrible snowstorm had claimed the lives of both my parents. They'd been victims of a car accident caused by a tourist who had been inexperienced at driving in the snow. The accident had taken her life too, but that hadn't felt like a consolation at all. My parents had been taken from this world too soon, and it had taken me years to rid myself of the hate and resentment. The pain and sadness of their loss was still there, but I've managed to learn to live with those dormant emotions that made random appearances every now and again.

With that horrendous loss, I'd been willed everything that my parents had owned. Being the only child, it had all fallen in my lap, including my father's construction company. Daniel Raynes had been the muscle behind Raynes Construction and Sela Raynes had been the brains behind everything else. My parents had been a phenomenal pair, and I could only hope that they were that same dynamic duo up in Heaven.

It had been a struggle to deal with my grief and the change of direction in my life, but my best friend and childhood buddy, Trevor Craig, had done his best to get me through those dark, struggling times. I'd just graduated from college and had been ready to move to New York and start my life as a financier. I had obtained degrees in business and finance and had been ready to take on the world. However, with the loss of my parents, maintaining what my father and mother had built mattered more to me than a high-profile career in New York. Overnight, my priorities had changed, and I've not regretted one day of my decision since then.

However, the need to sustain my parents' legacy had left me little time to do what most small-town folks did, and that was marry and have a family. The first three years after my parents' deaths, I had spent every waking minute learning the business from the ground up, and keeping the company from dipping into the red. I'd learned that the winter months consisted more of maintenance and repairs due to the harsh winters, and I'd learned that the summer months consisted of building the town folk's dreams as fast as I could while still giving them quality work.

While I had eventually gotten the hang of things and had felt comfortable enough to believe I was making my parents proud, the family thing had still been on the back burner of my life. Trevor had gone and married his wife, Karla, a few years ago, and they were working diligently on kids-or so Trevor liked to claim whenever I asked him why he looked so tired all the damn time.

As for me, I kept my dalliances casual and never with a woman from town. Brant was too small to date a local without the expectation of marriage after the second date.

No.

If I needed to get laid, I spent the weekends in Grand Forks or one of the other larger neighboring towns. It was less messy that way. Plus, while I didn't have any objections to getting married, it was hard to date women you've known all your life and looked at as sisters.

Still, I knew, sooner or later, that I was going to have to get onboard with some serious dating. I just wasn't in a hurry yet. I was only thirty. I still had a good five years left before I'd started to feel the panic about my own mortality.

"Be careful. You might get your suit dirty." I didn't even turn around. I stuck my arm out behind me and greeted Trevor with my middle finger. I heard his chuckle. "You're such a charmer."

I smiled, finished measuring the stud gap, then turned around. "What the hell are you doing here?" I asked. "Because you sure as shit weren't invited."

Trevor smiled, showing me all his perfectly straight teeth. "I don't need an invitation," he retorted. "I'm a goddamn delight. I know I'm always welcomed here." Trevor Craig was not a goddamn delight, but he was always welcomed here.

I pulled the hand towel from my back pocket and wiped my face. "No," I countered. "Your *wife* is a delight, and *she's* always welcomed here."

This time, he flipped me off but was smiling as he did it. "Seriously, though," he teased. "When are you going to get it through your thick head that you're the boss, Xan? Hire someone for this shit."

I was currently working on extending my personal home shed, and I was *not* wearing a suit. "Probably because all my guys are currently getting their asses kicked by three different projects that need to be finished by the time the first clouds start to roll in," I replied. I reached down, grabbed my bottle of water, then took a swig, before adding, "Besides, it's a goddamn shed, Trev. If I can't do something like an addon to my shed, I have no business wearing that suit you know I don't ever wear, asshole." He just smirked. "So, what are you doing here?"

Trevor just let out a rough laugh, and I eyed him as he ran his hand over the back of his neck. A nervous gesture, for sure. "Uh, I stopped by to invite you over for dinner," he answered anxiously, and my guard shot up like a cannon.

I narrowed my eyes at him. "Since when have you ever come over to *officially* invite me over for dinner?" I asked. "Usually, one of you just shoots me a text with an open invitation."

Trevor ducked his head and grimaced. "Well…Karla's hoping to butter you up with all your favorites so-"

"No," I said, stopping him. "No, no, no, no, no, Trev." I shook my head for emphasis. "I am not letting her set me up with another blind date th-"

The asshole laughed. "No, no," he chuckled. "It's nothing like that."

"Sure, it's not," I deadpanned. Karla had an unreasonable fear that I was going to die a lonely, bitter, old man, even though I've assured her that wasn't the case.

Trevor stuck his hands in his front pockets and just smiled. "I swear," he promised. "While she *is* going to try to butter you up for a favor, it's nothing like that."

I cocked my head at him. "What is it, then? A new addition to the house? A remodeled kitchen? A better-looking husband?"

"Fuck you, dude," he snorted. "I can remodel a kitchen on my own, you know."

I laughed. "What does she want, Trev?"

He shook his head. "Nu uh, buddy," he replied. "This is Karla's deal and I'm not going to end up in the doghouse because I ruined this for her." Trevor kept shaking his head to emphasis his convictions.

"I swear to God, Trev, if I show up and there's a woman there, I-"

He threw his hands up in surrender fashion. "I swear, Xander," he laughed, "it's nothing like that."

I planted my hands on my hips and regarded my best friend. "Does she need a kidney or something?" I asked, narrowing my eyes at him. "She doesn't have to ply me with my favorites if she needs a kidney or something, you know."

Trevor's stupid grin widened. "As far as I know, all her major organs are working fine," he volleyed. "But it's good to know that yours are up for option if that ever changes."

I threw my sweaty rag at him.

The lucky bastard saw it coming and side-stepped the assault. "Just…just be there, Xan," he pleaded.

I let out a sigh.

Trevor has been my best friend since forever, and when he married Karla, she had become my best friend-in-law. It helped that she was a sweetheart and never felt threatened by my close friendship with her husband. She had embraced me as her friend, too, and the rest was history.

"What time?" I asked, resigned to knowing that I was never going to deny Karla in the first place.

"Around six," Trevor replied as he turned to head back to his truck. "Nothing fancy." I grunted as his laugh faded, getting into his truck.

Brant, North Dakota didn't do fancy. The fanciest thing we had here was a water fountain in the middle of town square that a tourist had donated some five years ago or so. The woman had fallen in love with our 'quaint little town' and had just *had* to add to it. It was a nice fountain, but it didn't do anyone any good during the winter months when it would freeze over.

Turning back to the shed, I knew I had to move some ass now. I'd been planning on working into the night, but now that I was expected for dinner at the Craigs', that was a no-go. I set my phone alarm for five, picked up my measuring tape and leveler, then got back to work. It wasn't until my alarm went off that I started to wonder what the hell was so important that Karla felt she needed to ply me with rib-eye steak, mashed potatoes, asparagus, and whiskey. My stomach started growling at the thought, and I realized, it didn't matter. A home-cooked meal was a home-cooked meal.

CHAPTER 3

Fallon ~

I wish I could say I'd gotten some quality sleep, but that'd be a lie. My nerves had started firing like an electric storm the moment I had produced my I.D. to secure my roadside motel room in Montana, and they had stayed firing all night long.

Over the years, all I could conclude was that whoever was stalking me had to work with computers or law enforcement in some fashion. How else would they constantly be able to find me? After the second time I'd had to move, I had suspended all my social media accounts. I had limited all my internet use, and I'd naively believed that would be enough to save me.

It hadn't been.

Since the police couldn't-*or wouldn't help me*-whenever I wasn't working, I'd spent all my free time researching stalking, both the victims and perpetrators. The more I had researched, the more alarmed I had become as I realized just how easy technology made things for a stalker.

Our information was *everywhere*.

Even if you changed your name, a good hacker could find that out. Hell, a mediocre hacker could find that out. That, along with the part in me that was still a fighter, were the reasons I hadn't resorted to changing my identity just yet. Sure, I was scared. Sure, I lived in a constant state of paranoia. Sure, I'd had to upend my life constantly and start over. Sure, I was living like a scared rabbit. Still, I wasn't quite ready to wave the white flag just yet and let this...*person* drive me into losing my identity altogether.

Moving and starting over was akin to running, but it wasn't giving up. It was an attempt at a better life and a tribute to hope that he or she wouldn't find me again. Changing my name would feel too much like letting my stalker win. Sure, they were winning the battles, but I was still forcing them to engage in the war.

I was still fighting.

I wasn't necessarily winning, but I was still fighting.

Handing my I.D. over to the clerk had been nerve-racking, but I'd convinced myself that, even if he did find out that I'd been in Montana, he couldn't know if I was still there or had moved on. Maybe he would give me some credit and think I was trying to outsmart him by showing up in Montana but ending up in Florida.

God, please let him think I was in Florida.

It wasn't until I was secured inside the motel room that I realized just how bad my paranoia had sparked this time around. There was no way he could find me this quickly, and even if he did, he's never made his presence known right away. He always bade his time. Of course, this was the first time I've left California, so who knows what that might trigger in this psychopath.

However, I still felt the unrest of the last six years burrowing inside every muscle in my body. The aches of stress, paranoia, and fright were so embedded in my body that I no longer knew how to exist without them. If I woke up one morning feeling wonderful, I wouldn't know what to do with myself.

Before checking out of the motel room this morning, I had walked over to the lot next door where it housed a quaint little diner. I had eaten a quick breakfast, gone back to the motel, gathered my stuff, and then had checked out. Now, I was sitting in my car, ready to finish my road trip and get to Brant. I pulled out my cheap disposable cellphone and dialed the only number I knew by heart and have dialed for human interaction for six years.

Karla answered on the third ring. "Hey, girlie," she greeted. "How's the drive going?"

"It's good," I answered. "I was going to try to drive all the way through, but I thought it'd be best if I took a breather. I don't need to be on the road sleepy and desperate. Not a good combo."

"No, it's not," she replied softly. "When can I expect you?"

"Probably super late, Kar," I told her. "I'm sorry I didn't plan this better b-"

"Stop it," she chided. "You know it doesn't matter what time you show up."

"Well…" I hedged. "I…uh, was kind of thinking that maybe I should keep driving and make random motel stops until I get to Wisconsin. I can backtrack by sleeping in my car."

"Fallon," she gasped in a universal mom voice, "you know damn well how dangerous sleeping in your car is."

"I know…but I feel like, I don't know…like I need to do more to throw him off my track," I reasoned. "And I'll make sure to sleep somewhere safe. Or…maybe, I can plead with a motel owner, and tell them that I'm fleeing from my abusive cop husband or something."

Karla's sigh sounded worrisome. "Do…do whatever you feel you need to do, Fallon," she relented. "I just want you to be safe."

"I know," I replied because I really did know. Karla's concern for me was genuine and I felt guilty for bringing my drama to her doorstep, no matter how much she welcomed me. "I would just feel better knowing that I did my best to keep this from...tainting you."

She huffed. "Do not worry about me, Fallon," she scoffed. "I have Trevor, and he's enough to make me feel safe."

My heart panged with envy. I haven't dated since the second time I moved and Rob, my boyfriend at the time, had dumped me because he said my level of crazy exceeded that of most girls.

Normal girls.

After that, my need to be a part of someone had waned to the nonexistent need it was now. Having no faith in the police, no faith in men, and the refusal to endanger possible friends, I had started living a solitary existence. I had worked where I could get a job but kept to myself. Sure, there were moments of loneliness, but with fear and paranoia ever present, those brief moments didn't last long.

"Well, I figure I could arrive at your place tonight, sleep for a few hours, drive to Milwaukee, which is only nine hours or so, then dive back. That'd be an eighteen-hour drive. That's not too bad."

I could hear Karla hemming on her end of the phone. "Hmm, that could work," she reluctantly agreed. "You could probably even drive a little further and stay the night somewhere else in Wisconsin, giving off the impression that Wisconsin is where you're looking to settle down."

"I can probably go a little south and stay my final night in Indiana," I said, thinking out loud. "It could work."

"Hey," she burst out, suddenly sounding positive, "since it's summertime and I'm not working, I could totally ride with you. We can take turns driving, and that way, it will cut your travel time in half."

"Karla, I can't ask you to do that," I told her, immediately refusing her offer. I've never met her husband and the last thing I wanted to do was involve his wife more than I already have.

"You're not asking me," she pointed out.

"Besides," I cut in, "I have no idea who this person is or how they are able to find me. The last thing I need is to...set them off if they think I'm with someone. Stalking me might not be enough if they think someone is helping me."

"Okay, okay, okay," she rushed out. "It was just an idea."

"No, no, no," I quickly said. "I love that you offered, but...Karla, you have no idea the guilt I feel at dragging you into this. I'd rather...I'd rather keep you out of the fray as much as possible."

"Fallon, you're my friend," she whispered through the phone. "You've been my friend since we were children. You got me through some of the worst times in my life."

"The same goes," I told her. "I just...I need to feel that I can control *some* of this, you know. And that includes how I limit how much this touches those around me, especially you."

"Okay," she mumbled unhappily. "I get it, Fal. I do."

"Thank you," I breathed, feeling relieved.

"So, call me when you get here, and then you can catch up on some sleep," she said, reciting the plan. "Go do your extra drive, and when you get back, everything will be set up in the guest room for you."

"Okay, sounds good," I replied. "I'll see you soon, friend."

"I can't wait," she said, a smile in her voice.

"Okay, bye." She returned the departing remark before we hung up.

I turned the ignition to my grey 2009 Saturn Aura, and I was grateful it started. Now, it wasn't as if it was on its last leg or anything, but my money was hard-earned, and I didn't squander it. Once it had occurred to me that I might really have to spend my life moving from place to place, I'd made sure to save as much money as I could. Seriously, Scrooge would be proud.

I pulled out of the motel parking lot and merged onto the road, ready to move on. Since this was the first time that I've ever left California, my only hope was that my idea to drive to Indiana would work.

I couldn't say how long it took him to find me, but I'd usually be settled in for a few months before the oddities begin. Still, for all I knew, he could be tracking me nonstop, and he just bade his time because he was a sick fuck. I honestly had no idea.

I drove the rest of the way to North Dakota, going back and forth between lip-syncing to different varieties of music or listening to an audiobook. It wasn't until I checked my phone that I saw a text from Karla that was giving me something else to consider. I had texted her back to let her know I was going to keep driving until my eyes couldn't stay open anymore. I hadn't mentioned stopping in Brant at all.

I'd made it ten more hours before I pulled into the next motel.

CHAPTER 4

Xander ~

I stared at my best friend's beautiful wife with her strawberry blonde hair pulled back into a ponytail and her face free of bangs, showing off her sweet face. Those beautiful hazel eyes giving no hint to the crazy lurking inside her mind.

How could Karla be crazy, and I not have picked up on it until now?

And worse?

Trevor was sitting next to her, completely unfazed by the fact that his wife was crazy. I mean, looking at the guy, you could see that her insanity really wasn't fazing him in the least.

"I'm sorry, come again?" I asked as politely as I could. It always helped to deal with crazy people as politely as possible. I mean…granted, I haven't dealt with a lot of certifiable crazy people in my life before now, but it felt like sound advice anyway. Karla let out a soft sigh and her smile was timid, but I didn't think my reaction was unwarranted after sitting here listening to a story that had Hollywood written all over it.

No wonder she had made all my favorites.

"I know it's a lot to ask, Xander, but…you are the only person I could think of to ask," she sighed.

Karla and Trevor had refused to discuss the favor until after we had eaten, and now I suspect it was because I'd be too stuffed and fat to make a run for it. "You want me to purchase a house in *my* name, utilities included, for a friend of yours who is driving all the way over here from California because she's being stalked?"

"She would put up the money and pay the mortgage. She just can't have the house and stuff in her name," Karla clarified. "We don't know how he finds her, and for all we know, he could be a cop or someone good with computers. Fallon has no social media accounts and keeps to herself. The only way he can find her-after moving six times, might I add-is through her

15

work or rental information."

I ran my hands through my brown hair, making it stand on end no doubt, while I leaned back in the kitchen chair. Resting my arms back on the table I looked at Trevor. "Have you ever met this woman?"

He shook his head. "No," he answered. "She's a childhood friend of Karla's."

I gave him an understanding nod. I knew Karla was a foster kid, and that she moved to Brant after graduating from college where she'd met Trevor. His home was Brant, and this was where she had followed him. Her only family was an uncle who lived in South Dakota. Trevor was all she had here in Brant, but she seemed perfectly happy with that. This Fallon woman must really mean a lot to her.

I looked back at Karla and hated the words that were going to come out of my mouth because they were going to make it sound as if I didn't trust Karla, and that wasn't true. I trusted her almost as much as I trusted Trevor. Only difference was that Trevor had childhood friendship seniority on her. "So, you're asking me to take on a debt of hundreds of thousands of dollars on a...*promise* that she'll pay it? Are you really asking me to...risk my credit and financial reputation to...help out a stranger?"

Karla's back snapped and I could see her bristle a bit. "No," she contended. "I'm asking you to do me a favor, Xander."

My eye flicked towards Trevor before landing on Karla again. "If she's putting up all the money, why can't you guys purchase the home in your names?" I asked.

Karla let out another quiet sigh and her shoulders drooped, all offense evaporating. "The only thing Fallon's certain of is that it's someone from our childhood. She thinks it's someone who grew up with us in foster care."

"Because of the rabbit," I deduced.

Karla nodded. "Because of the rabbit," she confirmed. "It would be too easy to link my name to hers. Again, we don't know who it is, but it wasn't a secret that I was her best friend back then. Plus, it's not a secret that I'm her only friend now. He or she could easily look up properties in my name and find her that way."

I grabbed for the beer next to my empty dinner plate and took a good, long drink. It was hard to wrap my mind around her words. I mean, I knew people got stalked all the time. I wasn't a complete moron. Still, to stalk someone for years without making a move? That seemed...odd.

"Then why move here if she can be connected to you? Why not move to...Florida or New York? Hell, if a person really wanted to get lost, New York would be the place to do it."

Karla shrugged a shoulder. "She said she's tired of running," she replied. "She wants to try her hand at a normal life for once. She said if he comes for her here in Brant, then he comes for her. Plus, I think she might just be tired of being alone." I saw her reach for Trevor's hand, and he automatically linked his fingers through hers.

I was having difficulty buying into the desperation of the story. I knew Karla was telling me the truth as she knew it, but some of the story had holes in it. Not calling Karla a liar, but I knew some of the questions I had could only be answered by the woman in question.

I had uncharitable images of a theatrical damsel in distress, and I wasn't comfortable with that. I wasn't an asshole. I did my best not to judge people or their situations, but then, this situation was calling to involve me. And since it did, I deserved answers, right?

"And the police can't help her?" I asked. "Maybe a gun or self-defense?" Karla lifted her chin a bit, and I could tell she was getting offended at having to defend her friend, but this wasn't a ride to the store she was asking for. She wanted me to tie myself to a complete stranger financially for hundreds of thousands of dollars. "What about security cameras?"

"She knows some self-defense but isn't comfortable with guns," she replied. "In the current state her mind is in, she's afraid she'd accidentally shoot someone out of paranoid fear."

"And cameras?" Security cameras were always the first line of defense against intruders.

I could tell Karla was getting frustrated with me. "Of course, she's set up cameras before," she huffed. "It's another reason she thinks he might be a cop or into computers because the feed is always messed up or erased. She's even tried old fashion recording cameras, but those always come up missing. It's like…" Karla let out a soft, sad chuckle. "It's like *he's* got a camera in her apartment and knows what to look for."

"Maybe he has a tracker on her car," I suggested. "How do you know he's not just going to follow her here?"

"I don't even think she's thought of that," she mumbled quietly. I watched as she jumped out of the chair and ran into the living room. When she came back in, her phone was in her hands, and her fingers were flying across the screen. "That would explain why he can find her no matter where she goes," she continued to mumble.

I waited until she was done firing off her text before saying, "I'm not saying I'm going to do this, Karla, but I'd have to meet her first. Talk to her."

She rolled those pretty hazel orbs at me. "Well, of course, Xander," she muttered exasperated. "You know, you're not the only person who would be taking a gamble here."

I leaned forwards with my arms on the table. "How so?"

"Fallon would be trusting you with everything she has," she replied. "She would have to trust that you won't just sell her house out from under her. Or rent it out. Hell, you could even take out a second mortgage on it or suck out all the equity." Karla mimicked my position. "You could literally walk away with every cent she has and leave her with nothing."

Now it was my turn to bristle and get offended. "I would never do that to someone," I stressed though clenched teeth. *"Ever."*

Her eyes rounded and her head reared back. "You don't think I know that?" she gawked. "Why do you think I'm asking *you* for this, Xander?" She leaned back in towards me. "Next to Trevor, you are the most honorable man I know in this town. You were the first person I thought of when the subject came up."

I felt like a fool and calmed myself. "I'm sorry," I rushed out. "I know you weren't trying to insult me, Karla."

"Look," she said, suddenly sounding tired, "Fallon won't be here until tomorrow evening or so. I'm sure she'll be exhausted and just want to rest. Why don't I set up something for the next day when you guys can meet? It'll be Saturday, so maybe you guys can meet for coffee at Beth's, or you can come here."

I glanced at Trevor who'd been quiet this entire time. "No thoughts?" I asked him, putting him on the spot.

Trevor shook his head. "I don't have enough experience with what Fallon's dealing with to have any helpful ones," he replied.

I looked back at Karla and thought about what she said. It made me feel marginally better thinking about Fallon taking on a big risk herself. It made me feel as if this could be legitimate. Still, I would still have to meet her first; get a feel for her. "How about I just come by here?" I suggested. "That way she's where she's comfortable and not surrounded by a bunch of strangers in an unfamiliar town."

Karla nodded. "Yeah, that sounds like a good idea."

The rest of the evening felt strained, and I hated it. Trevor and Karla were my safe place. I trusted them with my life, and I've always felt welcomed in their home. However, tonight felt uncomfortable.

I also had a feeling it was only going to get worse.

CHAPTER 5

Fallon ~

The cab driver pulled up to the curbside and I let out the breath I felt like I'd been holding in since I left Indiana, where the car salesman assured me that I was purchasing a perfectly reliable Toyota. Still, he was a car salesman; he couldn't very well tell me he was selling me a lemon.

The second I'd gotten that text from Karla, asking me if I've ever checked my car for a tracker, my heart had sunk to the soles of my feet. For all my paranoid ways, that thought had never occurred to me. That was one way to explain how he always found me, that's for sure. I could have just taken it to a mechanic and had them check it, but it had made more sense to get a new car since I was determined to get a new life. So, I had traded in my car for a cheap one that was barely functioning and let the car salesman keep the profit.

I also left the car in an abandoned car garage that looked two days away from being demolished. The car was in my name, and if he was tracking me through my financial footprints, he would know I bought a different car, and he would know I bought it in Indiana.

After ditching the car, I had met a woman at the bus depot, and pleaded with her to buy me a ticket west to Missouri, and from there, I'd caught a bus back north towards North Dakota. At both stops, I had managed to find a sympathetic woman and I had lied, making up a story about how I was fleeing from an abusive husband. Once I'd told them that, they'd been more than willing to help me out. I had felt bad about lying, but the more I thought about it, the more I figured I wasn't really lying.

I was fleeing from someone I felt was dangerous.

I had also sent Karla one last text from my phone to inform her that he'll never find me in Indiana. Even though I used a throwaway phone, I was careful with my texts. Any conversations Karla and I had that included details were done over the phone. Our texts didn't give off any information about where I was going ever. They were mostly checking in and asking if I was okay. If he were able to get to my texts, he would just think Karla was checking on me.

I left the phone in the car in Indiana and didn't bother to purchase a new one. I was lucky enough that the last bus I'd had to catch went through Brant, and while it didn't normally stop in such a small town, the driver had made an exception for me. I had quickly discovered that with Brant being such a small town, there were still functioning phone booths scattered around the town. I had called a cab and had given him Karla's address. I figured if Karla's plan worked out, I could throw a car and phone into the deal and live off the grid, but still be able to live.

And now, it was Friday evening, and I was paying and tipping the driver as I looked up at the lovely cottage-style home that Karla lived in. After the cab driver had taken my money, he'd gotten out of the car at the same time I had and had walked around to grab my bags from out of the trunk. I had two suitcases, one duffle bag, and a carryall bag. I didn't own much and the carryall I had strapped across my body had all the money I had in it.

I reached for the suitcases, but the driver slapped my hands away. "Don't you dare, Miss Fallon," he scolded. "That's not how we do things here in Brant." When he had pulled up to pick me up, he'd gotten out and opened the door for me. He had also introduced himself as Jacob while he'd taken his hat off and had actually dipped his head. I couldn't remember the last time I'd seen manners like that.

I smiled because he was just so sweet. "It's not?" I teased.

He shook his head. "Absolutely not," he emphasized. "My momma would come clean out of the grave and whoop my ass if a woman ever carried anything around me." I smiled because he looked to be in his late fifties, but the respect he had for his mother and her memory was sweet. "And I don't need that mean, strict, old woman coming back from the dead." He looked up towards the Heavens. "Lord help little Black babies everywhere because there's nothing like a pissed off Black woman who takes her child rearing seriously."

I laughed and I couldn't recall the last time I expressed such a genuine laugh. "Well, then, by all means, Jacob," I said with flourish. "The last thing I want to do is get you in trouble with your momma."

"Amen," he muttered before we made our way up the path and to the front door.

Jacob set the suitcases down and turned towards me as I knocked on Karla's front door. "I'm not the only cab driver in Brant, but if you need anything, you just give me a call, Fallon," he offered, handing me his card. "It'd be my pleasure to get you around town."

I wanted to hug this man.

This complete stranger, a stranger who was doing nothing but being a kind, decent human being, I wanted to hug. The only reason I hadn't was because I didn't want him reporting me to the police on my first day in Brant. Mostly, because I feared that if I did, I'd fall apart in his arms.

So, instead, I smiled up at him and said, "Thank you, Jacob. You will definitely be on my speed dial as soon as I get a phone." He tipped his hat and turned back down the walkway as the front door opened.

"Fallon!" Karla squealed as he wrapped me up in her arms, then right in my left ear, she yelled, "Hi, Mr. Jacob!"

"Hi, Miss Karla!" he yelled back right before I heard the motor of his cab rumble.

Karla pulled back, and with her hands gripping my shoulders, her eyes ran the length of me. When her pretty hazel eyes moved back up to mine, they were shiny with unshed tears. "It's so good to see you, Fal," she breathed out softly. "I missed you."

I wanted to bask in this moment, but the underlining fear that shadowed my life was still there. "I missed you, too," I told her. "Why don't we..." I jerked my chin towards her front door.

Her face softened and understanding dawned in her eyes. "Of course, Fallon," she said before reaching for one of my suitcases. I grabbed the other one and followed her inside.

We headed inside and I stepped into the living room, looking around at Karla's home. You could tell right off that it was a home and not a house. It had personal touches everywhere.

"You have a lovely home, Karla," I told her.

She smiled and it reached her hazel eyes. "Thank you, Fallon," she replied as she glanced around the room. "It's...I'm happy here." I nodded and the moment passed. "Let me show you to your room." I followed behind her, and she led me down a short hallway that was lined with photos of Karla and her husband. There were pictures of vacations, outings, etc.

We got to the first door on the left and Karla opened the door. We walked in and it was a cute set up. It looked exactly like a guest room should look. "Here it is," she beamed as she placed my suitcase on the floor next to the full-size bed.

I placed the suitcase I was carrying next to the foot of the bed and dropped my purse, duffle bag, and carryall on top of the bed. I turned to face Karla. "Thanks, Karla." I shook my head. "You don't have any idea how much this means to me."

She threw her hand up to stop me. "Fallon, I know you feel guilty for coming here. I know you think that you'll somehow bring drama to my life, but I don't care. You're my friend and you've been handling this on your own for way too long." Her words caused a pang in my heart. "I can't count how many times you saved my life and my sanity growing up. Let me do this for you."

I took a deep breath and nodded my head. I wouldn't go so far as to say that I saved her life growing up, but when you had to grow up in a world where no one wanted you, it was easy to contemplate ending it all. I imagined that's what she meant.

I smiled for my friend. "Thanks, Karla," I replied. "Hopefully, your plan works, and we'll all be drama-free."

"Well, I'll let you get settled, and then we can catch up on everything we've missed." She smiled again as she added, "I already spoke with Xander, and he's agreed to come over tomorrow afternoon, so you guys can meet."

I inwardly cringed at her words.

Karla's plan was simple. She claimed her husband's best friend was the most honest man she knew-aside from her husband-and that her plan was sound. See, her plan was this: Xander Raynes would put my entire life in his name financially, and that way I could live life off the grid and the odds of finding me would diminish greatly. Karla promised that he was a decent guy, and I could trust him not to make off with everything I owned-but didn't own.

Over the past six years, I've managed to save about eighty-thousand dollars, and I was looking to buy a small home or use most of it for down payment on whatever I could find. I planned on finding a cheap, used car, but even then, I was finding Brant to be small enough that I might be able to get away with not having a car. Of course, I needed a job first before most everything else.

For years, I've fought this…invisible monster on my own, and the first time that I agree to lean on someone for help, it was a complete stranger who owed me nothing.

I trusted Karla, though. I had to accept that if she said this guy was trustworthy, well then, he must be. Still, what about his wife? Did he have a wife? Kids? I was entrusting my life to a complete stranger and that was probably just as frightening as living in fear of someone coming for me.

I said the only thing I could say. "Thanks, Karla. That sounds good."

Her smile remained. "I'll let you get settled," she replied as she walked out of the room.

Ironic words, considering that I didn't think I'd ever feel settled.

CHAPTER 6

Xander ~

I cut the engine off after pulling up to the curb in front of Trevor's house, and I swore a blue streak-*again*-for even showing up.

It's been a shitty day, and sitting here, I realized that I really didn't want to do this.

I mulled over everything Karla had said, but at the end of it all, I'd be tying myself to a complete stranger financially. Even if she did pay for everything, I would still be taking responsibility for someone who was embroiled in some seriously heavy drama. And after a supplier trying to fuck me earlier today, that didn't sound enticing *at all*. The love of money was the root of all evil for a reason.

Not to mention, if I did do this, what would happen if I did meet someone that I wanted to get serious with? What then? How would I explain this crazy situation?

I took a deep breath and steeled myself for the conversation I promised to have. I had given Karla my word that I would hear her friend out and really give this proposition some serious thought. And I would. *I have*. It's all I've been thinking about. However, I still couldn't shake the twinge in my gut telling me that I shouldn't get involved in this mess. My instincts were telling me not to borrow trouble when I didn't need to. I had a great life. Why would I risk fucking it up for a complete stranger?

I got out of my truck, click the key fob to lock it, then made my way up the walkway to the front door. I've been here a million times but, right now, I felt like a formal guest. I felt like I was here officially, and the feeling left a lot to be desired.

I rang the doorbell and waited until Trevor or Karla answered. A few seconds later, Trevor was opening the door, and that told me they were already in there waiting on me.

Trevor smiled. "Hey, man."

I gave him a quick nod. "Hey," I greeted back.

I watched as his eyes sliced to the side, then he closed the door tighter behind him before facing me and saying, "Look, Xander, before we go in there, I just want you to know that there will be no hard feelings if you say no to this."

I wasn't too sure about that, but I nodded anyway. I knew Trevor wouldn't hold it against me, but I wasn't too sure about Karla. "Okay. Sure, man."

He grimaced a bit before opening the door all the way, then stepping aside, so I could enter. "We're all in the back," he said. "On the deck."

Since I knew my way around, I didn't bother with letting Trevor lead the way. I just started walking towards the back of the house and he followed. Once we got to the sliding glass door that led out onto the decking, I slid the door open, and the two women immediately stood up from their chairs.

Karla smiled at me and walked over, engulfing me in a hug. "Hey, Xander," she greeted. "Glad you came."

Hugging her back, I leaned down and kissed her cheek. "Hey, Kar," I replied.

She stepped back, then reached over to pull her friend next to her. Looking back and forth between us, Karla made the introductions. "Xander Raynes, I'd like you to meet my very good friend, Fallon Reese." She reached behind Fallon and rubbed her back. "Fallon Reese, I'd like you to meet Xander Raynes. He's Trevor's best friend and my friend, as well."

Fallon's arm shot out as she reached over to shake my hand. "Hello, Mr. Raynes," she said. "It's nice to meet you."

I understood why we were here, but I wouldn't be a man if I didn't notice how attractive Fallon Reese was. She stood about five-foot-five-inches, and from what I could tell with her clothes on, she seemed to be perfectly proportioned to fit her frame. She didn't have over-exaggerated tits or ass. She had a delicate hourglass figure that boasted of anatomical perfection.

However, her stature was the only thing ordinary about her. Her fucking face was stunning. She had ink-black hair and ice-colored eyes. They danced back and forth between light blue and grey. They were framed by dark lashes, and they sat underneath a perfectly plucked set of brows. She had a delicate nose that sat perfect between two rosy cheeks, and her lips were evenly plump. There was no denying that Fallon Reese was beautiful if a little tired looking.

I took her hand in mine and her small hand was immediately swallowed whole by my hold. "Hi. It's nice to meet you," I repeated. "And you can call me Xander."

She pulled her hand out of my grip and I felt a quick stab of irritation, but I ignored it as she said, "In that case, you may call me Fallon if you don't think it will interfere with...uh, business."

My irritation inexplicably spiked at her choice of words. "I-"

"Why don't we all sit down," Trevor suggested, cutting me off. "Do you want something to drink?"

I glanced over at him as the girls returned to their seats. "Yeah," I answered. "A beer. Whatever you got." He nodded and went back into the house as I turned to eye which seat I was going to take. I opted to sit next to Karla, directly across from Fallon, so I could read her face as we spoke. I needed to absorb as much as I could about the woman and her situation.

Trevor came back outside with my beer, and after handing it over to me, he sat next to Fallon. Trevor was sitting directly across from Karla, and I was sitting directly across from Fallon. I wasn't sure how the girls felt about the seating arrangement, but that was the least of our problems. This shit was uncomfortable as hell.

Karla finally spoke, trying to ease the awkwardness. "So...uhm, I only told Xander the basics," she started. "I...uhm, felt it would be better if you answered his questions directly instead of third party."

Fallon gave Karla a small nod before turning that powerful gaze my way. "What questions did you have?" she asked, simple and direct.

"You're positive you're being stalked?" Fallon's entire back snapped straight, and I knew I had hit a nerve.

A big one.

However, she recognized her immediate response to my question, and I watched as she took a deep breath and said, "I apologize. I'm a little sensitive when it comes to that question." I didn't comment, but she went on to elaborate. "I've dealt with a lot of...unhelpful police officers in the past and that question puts me on the defensive."

I had thought it was a fair question, but I could see how indelicate the delivery might have been. I should have just listened to her story before raising doubts about it. "I'm so-"

"No," she said, shaking her head and interrupting my apology. "With what is being asked of you, you have the right to ask that question." Fallon shrugged a shoulder. "Any question, really."

I leaned back in my chair and took a drink of my beer. After swallowing, I repeated the question. "So, are you sure you're being stalked?"

"I've never lived with anyone before," she replied. "And after the first two years of...this, I stopped inviting friends to my home. No one ever came over and very few people knew where I lived, no matter where I was living. Plus, with every move to a new place, I would come home to find something in my apartment moved or messed with." She let out a humorless chuckled. "And I don't believe in ghosts, Mr. Raynes."

We had just given each other permission to use our first names, but she's chosen to call me Mr. Raynes. That meant she knew I was going to say no, or she wasn't going to trust me beyond this arrangement.

My irritation level spiked again.

I wasn't so clueless as not to realize that we'd seen right through each other the second we'd shaken hands. She knew I wasn't going to believe her and do this, and I knew she wasn't expecting me to.

"Karla's explained about how your cameras never seem to work, and she also mentioned that you're not exactly comfortable with a gun," I remarked.

Fallon nodded in agreement. "I think he might be into computers or something because my feeds are always corrupted. And she's right about a gun. Though, I have nothing against them, I just don't think I'm...calm enough to be responsible with one."

"And the police have never found fingerprints or...anything like that?"

"Contrary to popular belief, the police don't go to great lengths for victimless crime," she answered with a little bite in her voice. She obviously felt let down by our men in blue. "I've never been attacked, and nothing has ever been stolen, Mr. Raynes." That 'Mr. Raynes' crap was really starting to annoy me for some reason. "After all these years, it's still just my word that something is amiss."

"And you think living off the grid, with nothing in your name, will finally get you free of this person?"

"Nothing else has worked so far," she replied. "And, right now, I don't have a better idea. I've moved too many times to count, and he or she still finds me. Do you have a better idea?"

I didn't. However, this was all new to me, so it wasn't like I've ever given it much thought. I've never had a stalker or have stalked someone. I didn't know the first thing about taking precautions for something like this. Still, I did find it strange that someone obsessed with her enough to stalk her for years has never attacked her.

I stared at this stunning woman in front of me, and I knew I wasn't going to help her.

I couldn't be sure it wasn't all in her beautiful, crazy head.

CHAPTER 7

Fallon ~

He wasn't going to help me.

I knew it the second that we'd shaken hands.

He looked at me like he already knew I was more trouble than I was worth. There was no logical reason for him to invite drama into his life, and I didn't blame him. I just resented this little song and dance he was insisting upon when he knew he wasn't going to help me.

I doubt he ever was.

"I'll admit, I've never had to deal with something like this, so, no, I don't really have any…informed ideas on the subject," he answered.

I began to digest his words but quickly stopped. His words didn't matter at this point. Besides, it was probably a good thing that he wasn't going to help me.

When Xander Raynes walked out of the house onto the deck, I couldn't help but notice how hot the man looked. He was tall, even by men's basic standards. By looking at him, he had to be a couple of inches over six-foot. He had rich, dark brown hair and light brown eyes. His eyes were bright and intense, and a person could easily get lost in them. He filled out his button-up and jeans beautifully, and his sleeves were rolled up to showcase muscular, sinewy forearms.

He had a straight nose with sharp cheekbones, and his jaw was strong and pronounced. It worked for him. It all worked for him. Karla had mentioned that he was thirty-years-old, and that looked about right.

He looked good.

The last thing I needed was to give into the possibility of an attraction that could easily occur between men and women simply for just being a man and a woman.

"Look, I understand this is…unconventional, and…" *Christ.* How did you explain something so personal to someone who didn't believe you or didn't care to try? "I know this is a lot to ask."

Xander cocked his head, and his eye narrowed a bit, studying me. "It's just…difficult to grasp that someone has been stalking you for *years*, and yet hasn't made a move to…I don't know. Isn't the point of stalking someone to *eventually* get to them?"

"Sometimes, it's about the hunt," Karla said, chiming in. "I've read up on it, and the studies say that sometimes the stalker is obsessed with the fantasy and not the reality. If he makes himself known, then he no longer has the upper hand. He can no longer get off on frightening her. Stalkers control their victims through fear."

I looked back at Xander. "The only thing I can conclude is that if he attacks me or makes himself known, then this all ends. Whether by him killing me or him getting arrested, it still ends. He's had a one-sided relationship with me for years. Maybe he just doesn't want it to end."

He looked to be pondering my reasoning, but I knew it was just for show. He was obviously close to Trevor and Karla, so my guess was that he didn't want to look bad in front of them. Xander needed to go through the motions, so Karla wouldn't think he was a dick.

"So, how would this work, exactly?" he asked before taking another drink of his beer.

I took a deep breath and laid out Karla's plan. "I will look for a house I can afford, but you're the one who would buy it on paper. You'd have to be the one to meet with the realtors, banks, or mortgage lenders. The second that an offer is accepted, I'll give you most of my cash for a sizable down payment on the property. I'd give you money for all the deposits on the utilities and stuff, too."

He glanced over at Trevor, and I didn't like it. While I had nothing against Trevor, and even liked him, Karla was my friend. Karla was the one who knew what was going on. What could Trevor offer Xander regarding all this?

Xander looked back at me and asked, "Okay, so what about a job? I mean, you put your house and bills in my name, but you're going to have to work for a living, right? What's the point of doing all this when you're going to have to find employment under your real name?" Xander shrugged a shoulder. "Seems to me that if he is versed in computers or is a cop, he's going to be able to find you as soon as you land a job."

This was the part where things got tricky, and a might bit illegal. "I'm hoping that living in a small town there might be an opportunity to find something that's cash only and under the table, maybe," I admitted.

His brows shot up in surprise. "And if you can't?" he asked.

"I have enough savings to get me by for a while," I told him. "I was hoping to include a car in all this, as well. I could always find a job a couple of hours away if I have to. I don't mind a commute. I don't have a husband or kids, so the drive time won't take away from anything."

"So, now, there's a car in my name, too?" he asked, and no one could miss the irritation in his voice.

Before I could reply, Trevor stood up and said, "It looks like everyone needs top offs." He jerked his head towards the house. "Help me grab some more drinks, Xan."

I bit the inside of my cheek as Xander took the hint and stood up to follow Trevor into the house. This was turning into one of the most embarrassing disasters of my life, and that was saying something.

As soon as the sliding glass door shut, Karla reached over and patted my hand on the tabletop. "It's going to be fine, Fallon," she said unconvincingly. "He just...Xander's just trying to wrap his mind around everything."

I didn't trust myself to address her comments, so I took the coward's way out to buy myself some time. "I'm going to visit the restroom really quickly before they get back with the drinks," I told her, and then stood up to go into the house.

I shouldn't have lied.

I shouldn't have lied, and I should have stayed my ass outside with Karla.

I wasn't thinking about how I'd have to use the hallway that passed near the kitchen to get to the guest restroom. I didn't really think about it until I heard Trevor's and Xander's voices as clear as day.

"Alright, I admit, she's Karla's friend and I don't know much about her, Xan," Trevor was saying. "But Karla believes her, so-"

"C'mon, Trev," Xander replied. "Do you really believe someone's been stalking this woman for *years,* and the cops haven't been able to help her? It's like a bad Lifetime Original Movie. She was raised in foster care, only to have someone from her past-*suddenly*-start stalking her years later, but she has no idea who it could be." I heard the crack of a can open. "Then the dude's been stalking her for years by doing nothing but moving some shit around in her house?"

"Karla vouches for her," Trevor repeated. "That's good enough for me to have her in my house."

"Because you had a choice?" Xander countered. "And even so, Trev, it's not you or Karla who is putting themselves on the line for someone who is probably just crazy."

Trevor's voice sounded incredulous and genuine. "That's a bit harsh, don't you think?" he asked. "You just met her. Why do you doubt her story?"

"I know you're married and you're wildly in love with your wife, Trev," Xander replied. "But you can't tell me love and marriage has made you blind. That woman is beautiful. Do you really think if a guy were obsessed with her enough to stalk her for years that he wouldn't have made a move by now?"

"How the hell would I know?" Trevor exclaimed. "I'm not a stalker. How the fuck would I know what goes through a psycho's mind?"

"Fuck, Trev," Xander continued, not taking Trevor's questions seriously, "for all we know, her looks might be part of the problem. She could be doing all this for attention. How do we know this isn't just some scam she's concocted? There's probably a trail of abandoned sugar daddies lining the coast of California."

"Dude," Trevor said, sounding shocked, "I think you're being a bit...brutal here."

"I'm not being brutal," Xander denied. "I'm being realistic. I'm viewing this from the perception of someone who isn't emotionally involved with the situation. Karla's emotionally involved because they're friends, and you're emotionally involved because you love your wife and would do anything for her. I'm looking at the *facts.*"

"She seems sincere," Trevor mumbled.

I could hear the insulting arrogance in Xander's every word. "All sociopaths seem sincere. Narcissists do, too."

I expected surprise and some wariness from Xander Raynes. However, what I hadn't expected was flat out nastiness. According to Karla, Xander was supposed to be a good person with an open mind and a kind ear. How could she have gotten it so wrong?

There was a heartbeat of silence before Trevor said, "You're kind of being a dick, Xan."

"No, I'm not," he argued.

No matter what I was feeling, I wasn't going to let this continue. Karla had done me a huge favor by allowing me to stay in her home and forming a plan to help me. I wasn't going to repay her by letting her husband and friend become at odds over something that was ultimately my problem.

Besides, at this point, I wanted nothing to do with Xander Raynes. I had enough problems without being talked about viciously for no good reason. He could have simply just said no.

I stepped out from the hallway, and both men turned to look at me. Trevor looking startled and guilty. Xander looking apathetic. "Yeah, you kind of are," I said, agreeing with Trevor.

CHAPTER 8

Xander ~

I stared at Fallon, but what could I say? She overheard our conversation, and I wasn't going to further insult her intelligence by denying what I'd said.

"Fallon-"

She threw her hand up to stop Trevor from saying whatever it was he was going to say, but she kept her eyes on me. "You know, this wasn't even my idea," she informed me, surprising me. "Karla had come up with this idea, insisting that you were a decent person. She swore you were a good guy and a genuine person. But, boy, was she ever wrong."

"Fall-" Trevor tried again, but she just rolled right over him.

"I don't need you to believe me," she bit out, her eyes starting to water. "I don't need you to agree to this…strange arrangement. I don't need a fucking thing from you. Mr. Raynes. But…" Her voice broke as her hand waved back and forth between me and Trevor. "But *that?* That was unnecessary. I've never done a thing to you to warrant you talking so horribly about me." I couldn't lie and say I wasn't feeling lower and lower with each word she spewed. "You could have simply said no. That's it. That's all. When Karla brought it up, you could have simply told her no because you and I both know that you were never going to help me to begin with. You only agreed to this meeting, so Karla wouldn't see the real you."

Seeing her, unashamed and vulnerably open, made my heart drop. She was right. I was being cruel because I was in a shitty mood. Plus, all of this could have been avoided by simply saying no. "Fall-"

"Fuck you, Mr. Raynes," she hissed.

"Fallon." We had been so focused on Fallon's rant, none of us had noticed Karla walking in. "What's going on?"

Fallon turned towards her friend and let out an empty, dark laugh. "Your friend, you know, the one you swore was a good guy, a decent person? Well, I overheard him telling your husband that I had to be either crazy or a narcissist. That I made up this whole stalker thing up as a ruse to land sugar daddies to pay my way through life, didn't you know?" Karla's eyes flew to mine, and they were as wide as saucers.

"Karla-"

Fallon's dark laugh sliced through what I was going to say. "Yeah, Karla," she sneered. "He didn't want you to know that he really isn't a good guy, so he agreed to his meeting, so you'd still look at him through rose-colored glasses."

"Fallon, that's not what's going on," Trevor said.

Fallon ignored everyone around her and stepped up to me until she was forced to tilt her head back to maintain eye contact. "I don't care if you believe me. I don't care what you think of me. And I sure as fuck don't care what face you choose to show the world. You can just go fuck yourself, Mr. Raynes."

She went to walk away, and I wasn't sure why I did it, but I reached out and grabbed her arm. I couldn't just let this end like this. "Fa-"

Fallon wrenched her arm out of my hold so hard that she stumbled back. The look she gave me was pure, unadulterated *hate*. "Don't ever touch me again," she snarled, tears of hate and fury coursing down her face. "Just like no one has the right to...to enter my home without my permission. Just like no one has the right to pry into my life without my permission. Just like no one has the right to control me without my permission. No one has the right to *touch me* without my permission. No one has the right to terrorize me." I watched as she turned her back on us, then storm out of the kitchen, and I couldn't believe how torn up I felt over watching her fall magnificently apart.

"What in the hell is going on?" Karla hissed at both me and Trevor.

"Ba-"

I cut Trevor off because this was all me. "Don't get mad at him, Karla," I told her. "I was the one talking shit, not Trev."

Her pretty face fell in shock. "Why?" she asked. "Why would you talk shit about her? What'd..." Karla was genuinely stunned, and I felt like shit more so than I already had.

"I was...just trying to work it all out in my head, and...I wasn't watching my words," I lamely excused, but then thought better of it. "Okay, maybe I was being a bit dickish, but I wasn't trying to be cruel."

Karla looked hurt and that was gutting me. "I...oh, God," she cried out brokenly. "I promised her she was *safe* here." Her eyes darted back and forth frantically between me and Trevor. "I told her...I'm the one who told her to come here. *I'm* the one who promised she'd be welcomed and protected and you guys..." She placed a hand on her stomach like she was in physical pain. *"...oh, God."*

Trevor raced towards her. "Babe-"

Karla looked up at him, and she didn't even look mad, more like disappointed. "You don't understand, Trevor," she said, cutting him off. "Up until five minutes ago, I was the only person in her life that she had. I was the only person she trusted. I was the only person who hasn't let her down. I...she'll never trust me again."

This time, I stepped towards Karla. "I'm sorry, Karla," I told her, and realized how much I meant it. "I'll make it right. I'll-" Commotion in the living room cut me off and had us all heading into the room in time to see Fallon storming through the living room, all her bags in tow.

"Fallon-"

Fallon cut Karla off. "Thank you, for everything, Karla. Still, I'm not going to do this," she announced to the room. Then she looked over at Trevor. "Thank you for allowing me to stay last night."

Karla rushed towards her. "Fallon, it's all a big misunderstanding-"

Fallon smirked at her. "Their voices were loud and clear, Karla," she chuckled darkly. "There's no misunderstanding here." Fallon dropped one of her bags and wrapped Karla in a one-arm hug. "I love you, and I'm sorry if I caused any problems."

Karla pulled back. "Fallon, don't leave," she begged.

I watched as Fallon grabbed her bag, then turned those blue eyes my way. "I'm sorry I ever met you. And I'm really sorry people like you exist in a world where cynicism outshines compassion," she said evenly.

I stepped to her because I was very aware this disaster was entirely my fault. "Look-"

"Fuck you," she spat again, cutting me off, then heading towards the front door.

We all kind of stood stuck as she dropped her bag, opened the door, grabbed her bag again, and then walked out of the house. The second it was obvious that she wasn't going to shut the door behind her, Karla, Trevor, and I snapped out of our shock and raced towards the door. As soon as I cleared the doorway, I saw Jacob's cab idling by the curb. I watched as he jumped out of his cab when he noticed Fallon was carrying all her bags.

I knew I wasn't doing myself any favors, but I also knew that if I left things like this, the guilt would eat me alive, and I'd never be able to face Karla again without that guilt reflecting in my eyes. I raced down the walkway as Fallon and Jacob were placing her bags in the trunk of the cab.

"Fallon, wait a second," I said as I approached her.

She whirled around to face me, and I knew there was no way out of this. I couldn't undo the way she saw me. "Stay away from me, Mr. Raynes," she hissed, and I irrationally got irritated.

"Quit calling me that," I snapped.

Fallon ignored me. "Get away from me!" she yelled.

I stepped to her to-I wasn't sure what-but that's when Jacob got involved. He pulled her behind him, and his face was the most serious I had ever seen in all the years I've known Jacob. "Mr. Xander, Miss Fallon asked you to leave her alone," he repeated.

I felt Karla before I heard her. "Fallon, don't leave like this," she begged again.

Fallon's gaze shot towards Karla. "I still love you and I still trust you, Karla. But…I'm not going to stay, making your husband uncomfortable. And I sure as hell am not going to stay to be subjected to…whatever this is."

Before Karla could say anything more, Jacob had his arm wrapped around Fallon's shoulders and was shielding her as he opened the cab's rear door and ushered her inside. Jacob shut the door, finished placing Fallon's bags in the trunk, then made his way to the driver's side door. He gave me and Karla a terse nod of acknowledgment before getting in the cab and turning the ignition.

I stared down into the window and Fallon's face remained facing forward, her expression completely stilled. I watched as they drove off and the rock in the pit of my stomach felt like it was never going to go away.

"What the hell just happened?" Karla mumbled quietly.

I looked down at her. "I'm sorry, Karla," I said, and I meant every fucking word. "I…I'm not sure what got into me." Other than my fucked-up day that I had taken out on someone who hadn't deserved it.

She looked up at me. "I just don't understand, Xander," she replied. "You're not…you're not *that* person." She was right. I wasn't usually a cruel person. Even if I didn't believe Fallon, I shouldn't have been so cold about it.

"I'll find her and make it right," I said, promising the impossible.

Karla shook her head. "Just don't, Xander," she whispered. "She's been through enough."

Well, fuck.

CHAPTER 9

Fallon ~

What a disaster.

I had envisioned a lot of scenarios when Karla had set up that meeting, but I had never expected it to turn out this way. I had never expected someone that Karla called one of her best friends to turn out to be so awful.

Even without Karla's suggestion to entrust all my finances to…that man, the plan had been that I'd live in Brant. However, now, I needed to find a new place to try to live. I also knew I couldn't just stay in the back of Jacob's cab all day.

I didn't have a car or a place to stay, so no matter what I decided, I was going to have to show my I.D. for a motel room or a car I could sleep in. If I was going to show my hand, it made more sense to buy a car since I would need one to get around.

To run.

I leaned forward, and asked Jacob, "Hey, Jacob, is there a car lot in this town? I need a car."

I watched his shoulders hunch as if he were dreading ruining my day further by telling me there wasn't. "No, Miss Fallon," he answered, confirming my assumption.

"Do you know if there are any more buses coming through town tonight?" I needed to get out of Brant, that much I knew.

I watched the back of his head shake back and forth. "No, there aren't," he replied. "But I can drive you wherever you need to go." It was a sweet offer, and I respected how he wasn't prying, but I couldn't ask this man to drive me hours out of town. I wouldn't repay his kindness like that.

"Is there a cheap hotel or something in town?" I really didn't care about the price, but the seedier I could find, the more likely I could get by without showing any identification. However, Brant didn't strike me as the type of town that had seedy motels. The town really was picturesque.

"We have one bed and breakfast that Milly Sue runs, but we do have a motel on the edge of town that runs the highway for travelers," he replied.

No way in hell was I going to stay at Milly Sue's. "Can you take me to the motel on the highway, Jacob?"

"Of course, Miss Fallon," he whispered, and proceeded to drive me to the roadside motel.

As we pulled into the motel's car lot, I noticed a mini-convenient store on the right side of the shared commercial lot, and an understated tavern on the other side. It was actually a great place to stop for a rest if you were traveling. You could stockpile your road trip supplies and have a drink to decompress from a long drive.

Jacob pulled into an empty parking space right in front of the motel's office, but before I could get out, he turned around in his seat to face me. "Stay here," he instructed. "I'll go see if they have a room available, okay?"

I stared into Jacob's sweet, kind, brown eyes and actually felt wrecked that the world wasn't filled with more people like Jacob. I barely knew the man, but I had a feeling that Jacob always did the right thing because he didn't know how not to. He was kind, compassionate, and real. The world could do with a shitload more Jacobs, and a lot less Xanders.

I also realized just how close I was to having an exhausted emotional breakdown. Jacob's kindness was proving to be too much, so I just gave him a small smile and nodded my head.

After a few minutes, Jacob exited the motel's office with a key in hand, and I was stunned when he got back into the cab, then drove us further into the motel's structure. He parked in the empty space in front of a room that had 1045 on its door, and I couldn't keep quiet any longer. "Jacob?"

He turned around in his seat again to face me. "I'm not sure what is going on," he started, "but that...argument at Miss Karla's...well, I imagine you would probably welcome some privacy."

"But...I don't want to cause any issues," I stuttered. Jacob had a shiny gold band on his ring finger, and the last thing I wanted was for his wife to find out he had rented a motel room in his name for a complete stranger. Small towns were the horrible way of unfounded rumors.

Jacob smiled. "Miss Fallon, even if my wife didn't trust me completely, I called her when I was in the office and told her there'd be a charge on our credit card for Roadies' Motel." *Wow.* "She told me it was okay and requested that I be careful. Now...let's get you situated, yeah?" He didn't give me a chance to respond as he got out of the car, then headed towards the back of the cab to grab my bags. I finally opened the cab's door with shaky hands to help him.

We stood side-by-side with the trunk open when he handed me the keys to the motel room and said, "Go on and check the room out while I get these. I want to make sure you're happy with it before I leave you to it, Miss Fallon."

There was no way to stave off the emotional breakdown.

The tears started streaming down my face, and this sweet, sweet man gathered me up in his arms and just held me as I exhausted the past two weeks through a horribly undignified meltdown. "Now, now, Miss Fallon," he cooed. "Everything will look better in the morning."

I knew it wouldn't, though.

That's what he didn't know. Things wouldn't be better in the morning because I was still going to wake up in the morning tired, afraid, and lonely. Karla was right when she'd said that a stalker got off on inciting fear. I was at a crossroads where I was going to either keep living in fear or just let the person come for me.

I pulled back and smiled at Jacob through my tears. "Thank you, Jacob," I told him sincerely.

He smiled back. "Go on, now," he replied. "Go check out the room."

I did as he asked while he grabbed my bags, and I had to say that the room was nice as far as roadside motels went. I checked out the bathroom, and it was as equally clean and tidy as the room. Coming back out of the bathroom, I saw Jacob setting my bags on the bed, and once again, I was so grateful that he had been the person I'd chosen out the phone book. I was also grateful that Karla had still had a landline and Jacob's number had still been fresh in my memory, so I could call him after that disaster with Xander Raynes. I also still had his card.

"All good?"

I smiled and nodded. "I can't thank you enough for doing this for me, Jacob," I told him honestly. "Thank your wife, also."

Jacob's smile lit the room. "I'll be sure to do just that," he replied right before stepping to stand in front of me. His face took on the same seriousness I saw when he'd told Mr. Raynes to step back. "I'm not sure what you're running from, but I sensed you needed the anonymity of some…peace and quiet. While I don't believe Mr. Xander is dangerous, clearly, you just need some…breathing room." I took a deep breath because he couldn't be more right. "Call me if you need anything, Miss Fallon."

I shook my head. "You've already done so much, Jacob," I told him. "Let me get you the money for the room, and then you can-"

Jacob took a step back. "No," he argued. "There will be no paying us for the room. No one should have to pay back anyone for doing the right thing."

"But-"

"Miss Fallon, if we couldn't afford it, we wouldn't have done it," he stated firmly. "Just pay it forward, and all that."

"Thank you, Jacob," I repeated. "You don't know how much this means to me."

He cocked his head. "I have a feeling I do," he said gently. Then he threw me a quick wink and exited the room, locking the door behind him.

I dropped on the bed and tried to steady my nerves. I took a deep breath and scanned the room. As helpful as Jacob and his wife were, I knew I needed to make a decision about what to do next. All this motel room could do was give me a safe place to decided what to do next, but it didn't hold any answers for me.

I've been upheaving my life for six years already. Karla was my only friend, and even then, we'd only been friendly when I had felt it was safe enough to reach out to her. I haven't had a boyfriend in years, and the only sex I have had were quick, detachable, dirty couplings when the opportunity had presented itself, which, admittedly, hadn't been very often.

I also thought back to what Mr. Raynes had said. Why would someone stalk me for years and never make contact? Even if my stalker was getting off on scaring me, did he/she plan on scaring me for the rest of my life?

What was their endgame?

Plus, did I want to meet that fateful day with them calling all the shots, or did I want to finally put myself out there?

I knew I wasn't going to come up with an answer tonight, so I decided that I was going to take a shower, get dressed, and then head on over to the little tavern next door.

I needed a drink.

Hell, I needed to get drunk.

CHAPTER 10

Xander ~

Brant was the size of a shoebox, so it shouldn't be hard to find a goddamn stranger in this town.

However, apparently, it was.

Guilt was eating me alive, and while I still felt my concerns had been valid, everyone was right; there was no need to have voiced them the way I had.

I'd been a jerk-*no*. I'd been an asshole, and I could own that. The problem was that I couldn't find Fallon to apologize. I could squawk all day until the end of time about how I'd had a fucked-up day, but that still didn't excuse my behavior. Plus, it'd been more than just disappointing Trevor and hurting Karla. My parents hadn't raised me to mistreat people. And if they were alive today, they'd both be kicking my ass.

Plus, if I were being completely honest, my shitty day hadn't been the only thing to throw me off at Trevor's. I hadn't really given any thought to what Fallon Reese might look like, but when I'd walked out onto the back deck, I had been momentarily stunted by her stunning looks.

Fallon's hair was the darkest shade of ebony and it had been hanging loose around her shoulders, giving off a soft curl at the ends. Her eyes were a brilliant shade of light blue that were fringed by dark long lashes. When she stood up to shake my hand, I'd noticed that her body had been damn near perfection in her simple jeans and cotton t-shirt. Her tits were a handful, and her curves were femininely subtle. She had a realistic body; no plastic surgery turning her out like a cartoon.

No doubt about it, Fallon Reese was a beautiful woman, and that's why this whole stalker thing had thrown me off. Yeah, there'd been no need to be a dick, but the question of why this stalker hasn't attacked her yet was still valid. If I were obsessed with a woman who looked like Fallon, I wasn't sure if I'd been able to have stayed in the shadows as long as this guy has. Granted, I was assuming it was a guy, but who knew. Fallon had admitted to not knowing a thing about this person, other than they liked to torment her.

I ran my hands down my face, and I wasn't sure if I'd be able to live with this wretched feeling if I couldn't find her to apologize. I was sitting in the parking lot of Roadies' because I hadn't been able to find Fallon anywhere else. I'd even driven all over town looking for Jacob, but when I'd finally found him, he'd told me-in no uncertain terms-that he was going to mind his own business on this one.

Roadies' didn't have anyone registered under the name Fallon Reese, but if she were being truthful about everything, then I didn't imagine she'd get a room under her real name. If she'd been willing to let Karla talk her into handing everything she had over to a virtual stranger, my guess was that she was using a fake I.D.

The neon lights to Pit Stop's called to me in a way that only a man who has had a fucked-up day could appreciate. A shitload of alcohol sounded good right about now. I pulled away from Roadies' motel office and found an empty space in between the motel rooms and the bar. Roadies' and Pit Stop made a killing located on the highway, and travelers often extended their one-night stay into two. Brant was just that friendly.

I got out of my truck, locked it, then headed into the Pit for a beer.

Probably some shots, too.

If I couldn't find Fallon, I needed to drown this remorse. I walked through the door, and the bar was laid out like most hold-in-the-wall drinking establishments. The bar was right in line with the front door and ran the length of the west wall while the east wall was lined with dart boards, a shuffleboard, and a couple of arcade games. The restrooms were in the back, and there was a jukebox and a couple of pool tables near the back entrance. It was dimly lit, and the ambiance matched my mood perfectly. I gave the room a quick, slow, mildly curious glance as I walked towards the bar, and that's when I saw her.

Fallon was sitting at the end of the bar, a beer in hand, and a couple of empty shot glasses in front of her. My chest thumped with the idea of apologizing to a drunk Fallon because I couldn't imagine this would go well *at all,* but I wasn't a coward. And frankly, I deserved whatever scene she might cause. I walked towards the empty barstool next to her and sat my ass down.

Without saying a word, Darren placed a cold beer down in front of me and started a tab. It wasn't until he went back to cleaning the shelves that I finally spoke. It was still early, so the bar was fairly empty, but I did my best to keep my voice low, so the entire bar couldn't hear our business. "Look, Fall-"

She wasn't in the mood to hear it. "Darren?" she called out as she stood from the barstool. "Thank you for everything." I watched as she threw down a couple of twenties, and I irrationally wondered what the fuck he helped her with to warrant a tip that size.

Fallon headed towards the door, and I threw my own twenty down as a string of curse words left my mouth. "Fallon," I called out, but she ignored me. Darren's eyebrows shot up when I spared him a quick glance as I ran after her.

Small town gossip, just great.

I cleared the doorway, and whipping my head around, I saw the swish of a light green skirt round the corner of the building leading towards the motel. I ran after her, not caring who could see. Making a fool of myself in front of whoever might see was the least I could do to make amends.

Luckily, I was fast enough to see which door was hers, and when I got to her room, I pounded on the door like I had the right to. "Fallon!"

The door swung open, and her face was pure incredulity. "Are you crazy?" she screeched. "What is wrong with you?"

I muscled my way past her and into her motel room, even though I knew it was a dick thing to do. Something else to add to the list. I turned to look at her. "Look-"

Fallon still had the door open, and her face looked murderous. "Have you lost your fucking mind?!" she yelled. "Get out of my room!"

I crossed my arms over my chest in a show to let her know that I wasn't going anywhere. Well...unless someone called the cops on our argument. "I'm not going anywhere until we talk."

Her head reared back at my audacity, shock on her beautiful face. "Are you high?"

I shook my head. "I'm not crazy. There's nothing wrong with me, apart from some bad manners. I haven't lost my mind. And, no, I'm not high," I said, answering all her questions.

She finally shut the door, probably not wanting to invite anyone into our little drama just like I didn't, but she cocked her head at me and said, "You must be so high that you don't realize you're high because why else would you believe that I'd want to talk to you?"

I sighed. "Look, I wanted to apolog-"

She let out a dark, tired laugh. "You can take your apology and shove it up your ass, Mr. Raynes," she spat. "I give two fucks about your apology." She flipped her hand in the air as if she were dismissing me. "Go apologize to Karla and Trevor. Don't waste it on me because I don't care to hear it."

I stepped towards her, but instead of stepping back in trepidation, she drew herself up to her full height and stared me down.

I guess Fallon Reese was tired of running.

I was ready with my apology, but my mind detoured to something I couldn't ignore. "It's Xander," I reminder her, ignoring her words.

A perfectly arched brow shot up. "I don't care if it's Jesus," she replied coolly. "All I care about is you leaving me in peace."

She didn't want to hear an apology, but maybe she'd be willing to hear my offer. "Fallon, let me help you," I said, instead of saying sorry again.

She smirked, and it was ugly on someone so beautiful. "I don't need your help, Mr. Raynes," she replied, using my fucking last name again. "Like I told you before, this was all Karla's idea. I can get through this without you or your help."

Fuck, she was stubborn.

I stepped to her, so I was standing closer to her, but still respecting her space. "But you don't have to," I pointed out. "Just…just let me apologize and explain. Just hear me out."

This time, she crossed her arms over her chest-and because I really was an asshole, it was a fucking impressive chest-and eyed me. "Like I told you before," she bit out, "I am not interested in your apology or explanations, Mr. Raynes. I-"

"Quit fucking calling me that," I snapped without any right to. I knew I was in the wrong here. I knew that. However, I also knew I *hated* the way she called me by my last name.

Fallon stepped towards me, so that we were face-to-chest, and she glared up at me. "Fine," she spewed. "Is this better? Fuck off, *Xander.*"

I groaned. I knew she was going to be pissed and difficult, but I would think someone this desperate would at least hear me out. "Fallon-"

Then she surprised me when she asked, "Why don't you believe me?"

I looked into those pissed off blue eyes of hers and couldn't find it in me to lie to her. I probably should since I was trying to get into her good graces, but I just couldn't. "Because I can't understand why someone who is obsessed with you wouldn't have already made a move," I told her honestly. "You've got to be one of the hottest women I have ever seen. There's no way I'd be able to stay away if it were me, and *that's* why I'm struggling to believe you."

CHAPTER 11

Fallon ~
Holy.
Shit.

Out of all the things I had expected Xander Raynes to say, that sure as hell hadn't been one of them.

Suddenly, the motel room felt stifling. It felt smaller and...inappropriate. *I* felt smaller and inappropriate. I was being tormented by a madman, and I was literally on the run for my life, but all I could seem to think about in this moment was how a man as good-looking-albeit an asshole-as Xander Raynes was standing in my motel room, telling me that I was one of the hottest women he's ever seen. And that if he were my stalker, he wouldn't have the self-control to stay away from me.

I could admit that my dry spell was more like a two-year drought, but was I so desperate for human contact that a jerk like Xander Raynes was looking good right now?

I shook my head and snapped myself out of those dangerous and useless thoughts. Even if I did want a one-night stand with a man, I didn't want it to be with one who thought I was crazy. Or worse, an attention seeking whore.

Jesus. Get a grip, Fallon.

"That's your reasoning?" I replied, trying to aloofness.

He lifted his chin, and it was a shame he was such a good-looking sonofabitch. In another life, I might have liked this man. "I can't imagine any man who could stay away for that many years without just taking you, Fallon," he repeated, but this time, his voice carried a heat it hadn't before, and I knew Xander Raynes was a bad fucking idea.

Ignoring all my firing lady bits, I forced my mind to get back to the subject at hand. While the beers and tequila shots hadn't solved all my problems, they had helped me come to terms with a decision that was long overdue.

"Well, I no longer need your help, Mr. Ra-Xander," I replied. This was truly none of his business, but the sooner I told him about my come-to-Jesus moment, the quicker he could leave. He was here out of guilt, and as soon as he found out that he had nothing to be guilty about, he could move on with his life. "I've decided to stay. However, I decided to…do it in the open and face whatever awaits me." His back straightened and his nostrils flared like I just pissed him off, but my life wasn't his business or his responsibility.

He was quiet for a few seconds before finally saying, "Maybe a decision like this shouldn't be made after beers and shots." He sounded so condescending that I was back to wanting to punch him in the face.

"Quite frankly, my decision-*however it was made*-is none of your business," I told him, stressing that, yet again, my life was none of his business. "If he comes for me, then he comes for me. But at least, this way, I have Karla in my corner."

He looked like he wanted to argue the point, but instead he just gave me tight nod. "I'm really sorry I judged you the way I did," he said, and I wasn't sure what to do with that.

I had bigger issues to deal with besides what Xander Raynes thought of me. Sure, it'd be nice if we could get along for Karla and Trevor's sake, but I hadn't really planned on spending that much time with Karla and Trevor to begin with. As much as Karla *was* in my corner, I wanted to spare her from my drama as much as possible. I figured with getting a job and getting settled in, a once-a-week lunch or something like that would be good enough to still be friends but not put her in any harm's way. With the deliberate distance, the odds of running into Xander were slim to none.

I shrugged a shoulder as casually as I could. "Don't worry about it," I told him. "Now that I'm going in a different direction, what happened earlier doesn't even matter." I stared into those bright amber eyes of his. "Your opinion of me doesn't matter. It never did."

Then he surprised the hell out of me by saying, "Well, your opinion of me matters."

I glanced around the motel room and took inventory of my life before I looked back at him. "No, it doesn't," I corrected. "Karla's and Trevor's opinions of you matter, and I can understand that. However, this is where we part ways, Xander." He opened his mouth to argue, but I put my hand up to stop him. "Even if you are genuinely sorry, I have enough problems in my life without inviting someone who I don't trust into it. And, make no mistake, Xander, I don't trust you. I'll never trust you."

He dropped his head, then ran his hands through his chocolate-colored hair, swearing a string worthy of a sailor before looking back at me. "Just let me fucking explain," he growled.

I didn't want him to explain. I wanted him gone. I didn't need to be attracted to someone who thought so little of me and was so quick to judge. Hell, maybe I was judging him quickly and unfairly, too, but I wasn't being cruel about it. Plus, I was finding myself attracted to Xander Raynes, and the longer he stood in my motel room, the more likely that I'd end up making a grave mistake where he was concerned. A mistake I didn't need.

"I need you to please leave, Xander," I said, betraying nothing.

Xander shook his head in defeat, but then walked over to the nightstand. I stood at the door as I watched him write something down on the complimentary notepad by the lamp. He ripped the page off, then walked over to hand it to me. I grabbed it and saw that it was a phone number.

"That's my number," he said. "If you've decided to meet this situation head-on, I imagine you're probably going to get a real phone soon. That's my number if you need m-anything."

I was still hurt and insulted enough to want to wad up the piece of paper and throw it in his face, but I didn't. I didn't because I didn't want to make this situation any harder on Karla and Trevor than necessary. Xander was their friend and there was no value in being mean to him.

I stepped away from the door and place the paper on the edge of the bed. "Thanks," I replied, my back to him, but before I could turn back around to see him out, I felt his body heat envelop my entire body from behind. I couldn't disguise the hitch in my breath at his proximity. And while I should be feeling anxious that a virtual stranger was invading my space, all I felt was a dangerous longing, and not necessarily for Xander, himself. It's been ages since I've been with someone, and the one-night stands I did have hadn't left much room for affection. They'd mostly been encounters to relive the stress that was my life. They had also helped me not feel alone if only for a few hours.

This was different.

Xander wasn't a passing stranger. He was Trevor's best friend and a fixture here in Brant. I couldn't sleep with him, and then just walk away. Now that I've decided to make Brant my home, I had to treat the town and its people with the respect it deserved as my new home. Screwing the first guy who made my skin break out in chills was not the way to go. Once I got settled, I could drive over to one of the bigger cities to get laid if I needed to.

His breath was hot against my ear as he whispered, "I really am sorry, Fallon."

I closed my eyes and really wished I could have just held onto the hate I'd been feeling for him. I wanted to stay mad at him and believe he was only here for Karla's sake, but it was harder and harder to hold onto my righteousness the more and more he tried to apologize.

I took a step forward to give myself some much-needed distance from him, then turned to face him. "Let's just drop it, Xander," I replied. "We don't need to be friends, but we can still be cordial for the sake of Karla and Trevor." Before he could respond, I added, "Besides, Brant is a small town. There's no need to make enemies where there doesn't need to be."

He ran his hands through his hair again, a nervous trait, maybe. The look he gave me was one of pure frustration. "I was having a shitty day, Fallon," he said as a way of an explanation. "I shouldn't have taken it out on you."

I decided to take the coward's way out. "Look, Xander, it's been a long goddamn week," I said, ignoring his explanation. "I just want to get some rest before I have to tackle the next phase of my life on Monday." I wasn't necessarily lying.

He regarded me with eyes too pretty to belong on a man. "Okay, Fallon," he replied. "I'll give you this, but this isn't over."

Wow.

I cocked my head at him, trying to understand his game. "Which is it, Xander?"

"Which is what?" he growled.

"Are you the asshole who treated a stranger like shit? Are you the remorseful guy who wants to make things right? Or are you a dick who doesn't like to be questioned?" I challenged. "Because I gotta tell you, your many personalities are giving me whiplash."

Xander stepped to me, and I should probably take exception but for the fact that, if I was going to face down a stalker, I needed to toughen up. "I'm all three, Fallon," he snapped. "I'm the guy who had a shitty day, and acted like an asshole, but felt like shit afterwards and came to apologize. I'm also the guy who has no problem being a dick if it means people are *safe.*" Xander turned, then slammed the door behind before I could comment on his little rant.

What a day.

What a goddamn disaster.

CHAPTER 12

Xander ~

"Well, she didn't murder you on the spot, so I suppose there's that." As comforting as that should have sounded, it didn't. It was Sunday afternoon and Trevor was helping me with my shed. I didn't need the help, so I suspected he was here checking on me more than anything else.

I turned to side-eye the man. I had just finished telling him about the fight, or not fight, or whatever the fuck it was between me and Fallon yesterday. "Yeah, Trev," I said drolly, "that's a great plus."

He finished hammering the plank nails. "Xander, you were a fucking dick to her," he replied incredulously. "You're lucky you're in one piece, considering Karla would have stood back and let Fallon murder you."

I turned the saw back on to drown the motherfucker out, but he came over, yanked on the cord, unplugging it. "Hey, asshole, don't be doing that. It's dangerous," I grumbled.

He didn't listen. He just stood there with his arms folded over his chest. "I'll tell you what's dangerous, Xan, and that's two pissed off women. Forget a damn power saw."

I winced because I didn't like the idea of Karla being pissed at me. "Is Karla really pissed at me?"

Trevor let out a sigh. "No. I think she's more disappointed than anything."

The punch to the gut was real. "Jesus, Trevor, that's worse."

He just shrugged a shoulder. "Dude, don't look at me. I'm not the one who acted like a jackass."

Pushing work to the side, I looked at my friend, then asked the question that I was hoping he had the answer to. "How do I fix this, Trev?"

"C'mon, man," he said sympathetically. "You know Karla won't stay mad-"

"I mean with Fallon," I corrected. I knew Karla wouldn't stay mad at me forever, but that was because I had history with her working on my side.

47

Karla knew I was a nice guy for the most part. She wouldn't believe the worst of me and hold onto that. Fallon on the other hand…

Trevor's brows shot up. "Fallon?"

"Yes. Fallon. You dick," I snapped, my voice brittle.

"Well, well, well," he chuckled.

He really was a dick.

"I didn't think you cared that much," he taunted. "You know, seeing as how she's a gold-digging attention seeker, and all." My face must have conveyed what I thought about his remark because he put his hands up in surrender. "Sorry, man. I couldn't help myself."

"I already feel like shit as it is, Trev. Can you just not?" I knew I sounded like a whining brat, but I hadn't slept a wink last night, worried about how to make shit right with that girl.

Trevor took mercy on me. "Sorry, Xan," he sighed. "However, I really don't know much about the woman. She's Karla's friend, remember?" Which translated to 'you're assed the fuck out' because I knew there was no way Karla would tell me anything about Fallon at this point. I already made Karla feel as if she'd betrayed Fallon once already, there was no way Karla would help me with this.

"The guilt is eating me alive, Trevor," I admitted. "I feel like shit over the way I treated her."

Trevor reached for a bottle of water out of the ice chest. "But why?" He twisted the cap. "You told me that she said to just drop it and move on, right? That's close enough to forgiveness, don't you think?"

These next words were probably going to damn me, but Trevor was my best friend; I wasn't going to lie to him. "I don't want to move on," I confessed. Trevor started choking on his water and I had to wait until he pulled himself together before saying, "I don't want to pretend like she doesn't affect me whenever I might run into her with Karla."

"Holy shit," he choked out. I watched as he shook himself out of his stupor. "When the hell did that happen?" I couldn't blame his incredulity. "How did you go from trashing the poor woman to wanting to get her into your bed?"

"First and foremost, I'm a man, Trevor," I snapped. "I wanted her in my bed the second I laid eyes on her. She's fucking beautiful."

The asshole rolled his eyes. "Sure, she's beautiful, but since when did you ever fall stupid for a pretty face? You're more of a personality kind of guy."

This was getting me nowhere. "Does it matter? The fact is that, even if I didn't feel like a goddamn heel for misjudging her, I'm attracted to her in a way that I'm not sure I can ignore."

Trevor put the water down like it was a danger to him right now. "And you realized this when, exactly?"

I knew the exact moment I was fucked. It was when she finally said my name after telling me to fuck off. She was running from an unknown threat.

She was tired and scared. Still, even through all the shit that she's been dealt, she still had fire in her. She still had fight. Plus, she'd been alone in her motel room with a stranger, and she had still balled up and told me to fuck off.

Fallon wasn't manufactured.

She was real, and she was strong, and the regret of my actions had hit me hard in that moment. I had misjudged her horribly and my attraction to her had made my regret all that much more palpable.

"When she told me to fuck off," I told him.

"Jesus, Xan," Trevor chuckled. "You never do anything easy, do you?"

"You are absolutely no help, Trev. None at all."

He shrugged, knowing my conscience wasn't his problem. "I know Karla better than anyone, and even I don't know what to do with the woman when she's spitting mad. No man knows what to do with a pissed off woman, Xan. Keep groveling is all I can tell you."

I gladly would if that's all she required of me, but it wasn't. The woman wanted me to leave her alone, but I wasn't sure I could. Even if I wasn't attracted to her and she wasn't Karla's best friend, Brant was the size of a postage stamp. There was no way I'd not see her around town, and I didn't want to walk on eggshells every time I ran into her.

"Plug the damn saw back in, asshole," I mumbled as I realized Trevor was no help at all. The fucker laughed at me, but plugged the saw back in, nonetheless.

The sound of the saw drowning out everything else gave me the opportunity to wonder how far I was willing to go to make amends with Fallon. I wanted things to be cool between us, and Lord knows I wanted the woman in my bed, but there was still the whole stalking issue she was dealing with. I knew if I pursued her, I could very well be getting myself caught up in something dangerous and confusing.

The man in me could appreciate wanting her to be safe because she was a woman, and a woman should never feel anything but safe. However, the man in me down below took it a little more personally. If I got involved with Fallon, her situation would become my situation, and that was a bigger burden to bear that just putting a house in my name.

Then I had to laugh at myself.

I was thinking about all this as if getting involved with Fallon was a foregone conclusion. The woman couldn't stand me, and I was contemplating all the pros and cons of dating her.

Maybe I was an asshole.

Even if the attraction was mutual, Fallon had bigger things to deal with than some guy who'd been a jerk to her. She had real-life problems, and even if she wasn't being stalked by some lunatic, she was still moving to a new town, trying to get a job, and find some place to live. That was a lot to take on, even without the fear factor.

I meant what I'd told her in that I couldn't understand how someone could stalk her for so many years and not make himself known. There was no way I'd be able to stay hidden if I was fixated on her. That's why I had doubted her story, at first. Hell, I still couldn't fully grasp her situation, but I realized I wanted to. I wanted to help, and I also wanted to phase Karla out. If Fallon felt comfortable calling me, then that was one step closer to keeping Karla safe and away from whoever was tormenting Fallon.

Now, while I didn't have any problems with strong, independent, ball-busting women, I took my role as a man seriously, and with that, came the need to protect the fairer sex if I could. I had no doubt Karla and Fallon could probably take on the threat together, but the thought sent unpleasant tingles down my spine. Trevor would never be the same if anything happened to Karla. He lived for his wife and made no bones about it.

Just then, an idea started forming in my head. While completely ridiculous, it was worth a shot. All these years, he's been after a single woman living a scared, solitary life, but what if she had a boyfriend? What if she was living with someone? Would he still come after her? Would he still be so bold?

I made a mental note to ask Karla if Fallon has ever had a boyfriend since the stalking had begun, just to get a better picture of what we were dealing with. Sure, there was no way Fallon would move in with me or pretend to be my girlfriend, but that wasn't going to deter me. If she were willing to go along with Karla's plan to put herself at my financial mercy, then surely, she could see the value in a compromise of sorts, right? Granted, Karla's plan had all been before I'd treated her like shit and she hated me, but it wouldn't hurt to offer up my plan.

I mean, the worse she could do was tell me to fuck off, but she's already done that, so I was thick-skinned there. Right now, guilt and attraction were a lethal combination working to devise a plan that would help us both. Fallon from her stalker and me from losing my goddamn mind with worry and guilt.

CHAPTER 13

Fallon ~

He must do drugs.

That could be the only explanation for why I was at Karla's, listening to Xander Raynes and his insane idea.

I mean, I thought he might be a little touched in the head when he'd shown up at my motel room the other night, but this?

This was proof that he was doing drugs.

There was a heartbeat of silence before I turned to Trevor and said, "I know Brant is small, but surely, there are drug rehab programs available through the church or something to help Xander, Trevor. Because your friend is obviously on some heavy shit."

Trevor laughed at my remark while Karla chuckled softly. Xander grunted, not appreciating how I was trying to get him some help. I mean, I didn't care for the man, but that didn't mean I didn't have compassion for people with drug problems. Not all drug abusers were bad people. Some were good people just making bad choices.

Across the table, Xander leaned forward with his elbows propped up and his hands clasped together. A bit white-knuckled, I might add. "I don't do drugs, Fallon," he gritted out, clearly insulted.

"I beg to differ," I argued. "You must, Xander. That's the only reason why you would voice this ridiculous idea."

His amber orbs narrowed a bit. "Why is it ridiculous? Karla has pretty much confirmed that you've lived alone all these years since this all started. Who's to say my idea doesn't work?"

I cocked my head as my brows drew downward. As if addressing an idiot, I replied, "It's ridiculous because I can barely stand to talk to you, much less live in the same goddamn house as you."

"You're willing to shoot down a good idea just because you're still mad?" he asked.

"I'm not mad at you, Xander. I don't *like* you," I clarified. "There is a difference, you know." While I was woman enough to admit the attraction, that still didn't mean I liked the man. It just meant that he was hot as hell and looked like he knew what to do with a woman once he got her in his bed.

He seemed unaffected by my declaration. "Then this gives me a chance to change your mind about me while keeping you safe."

"And what about your safety? What if this guy comes after you?" The second those words flew out of my mouth, I knew Xander Raynes was a man's man. His entire demeanor shifted into alpha mode and the look on his face was positively feral.

"Let's get something straight here, Fallon," he growled. Honestly, truly growled. "I can take care of myself. I can protect myself just fine. And I sure as hell can protect you if it comes down to it. I wouldn't be suggesting you live with me if I didn't think I could."

Okay.

Well.

Time to incorporate some common sense into this insane scheme. "Xander, you don't know me," I pointed out. "You know nothing about me. It's crazy to allow someone that you don't know to invade your space." Having lived with the violation of someone coming into my home whenever they felt like it, my respect for people's private space was extreme.

Then he hit me with something I wasn't expecting. "Just like you were willing to hand over everything you own to me on the word of Karla's trust for me, I'm willing to trust you on her word as well."

The thud in my chest was real. Xander seemed as if he was trying, but that first impression was too hard to shake off. "And what if I leave the milk out? What if I don't put the cap back on the toothpaste? What if I let my laundry pile up? There are more issues here to contend with, other than me making off with all your valuables."

"I'm not a big fan of milk. You'll have your own bathroom. And I'll be happy to do your laundry." The last part was said with the smoothness of silk and a positively rakish look in his eyes.

"My own bathroom?" Not saying I was going to go along with this idiotic plan, but my own bathroom was a selling point.

Xander let out a small sigh while Karla and Trevor just sat next to us, watching in fascination. "My house has three bedrooms, one being with a master bath. That's my room. There's a guest bathroom that would be yours, and there's even a half bath off the kitchen."

"What are the other two bedrooms used for?" Again, not saying I was agreeing, but I wanted all the facts when I said no.

"One is a guestroom and the other was converted to an office," he answered, matter of fact.

The lonely part of me started to entertain the idea, so I shook my head to get rid myself of the lost longing feeling. "Look, Xander, I appreciate you trying to make amends, really," I told him honestly. "But this is a bit extreme in the effort." He started to object but I continued, cutting him off. "I have enough money to put down on a house if not buy one outright. I don't need to put anyone out."

"But why make that commitment when you don't have to?" he countered. "Why not move in with me and wait it out for a while. If he doesn't show up, then buy the house and settle here."

"Xander, sometimes he doesn't show up for over a year," I explained. "Besides, I'm done running."

Karla leaned into me. "And I'm glad," she whispered.

I was about to do my victory lap when Trevor spoke up. "Fallon, hon, even if you do have the money to put down on a house, buying a house doesn't happen overnight. There's still escrow and a whole host of other shit that needs to be done before you're handed the keys. Not to mention, if you're really going to do this, you're going to need to find a job and buy a car and whatever else. Do you really want to do all that living out of a motel room that's on the outskirts of town?" Trevor was beating me down with sensible logic, and I was not liking it. "Staying with Xander saves you time and money. And considering that you're going to blow a big chunk of your money on a house and car, you could probably stand to save as much as you can right now. The idea might sound crazy, but it's actually not a bad idea."

"But-"

Ignoring me because the man had logic as his superpower, he kept talking. "You could always stay here as originally planned, but staying with Xan gives you more privacy, and quite frankly, keeps Karla out of harm's way, Fallon," he finished honestly, and I appreciated it more than he could ever know.

I searched all their faces, and I could see they were all in favor of me staying with Xander. Still, just like Trevor was concerned for Karla, I was concerned for anyone who could get tangled in my mess. And that included Xander, even though he'd been a jerk to me in the beginning.

If I was going to be brave enough to stop running, I had to be brave *period*. I couldn't pick and choose when to be strong with this situation.

"I appreciate the offer and the reasoning, gentlemen," I told them. "But staying at the motel isn't a problem. I'm not a manicure/pedicure kind of girl anyway. A motel isn't on my list of hardships. And since I plan on getting a job, I'm not worried about the money."

"Fal-"

I stopped Trevor from whatever he was about to say. "I'm not going to hide behind Xander, Trevor," I said, my voice clear and strong.

"Are you fucking kidding me?" Xander exploded as he stood up from the table. He slapped his hands down on the tabletop and glared at me. "Are you seriously turning down my offer to be all 'I-am-woman-hear-me-roar'? Are you fucking serious?"

I stood up because...well, fuck this asshole, that's why. "I'm turning down your offer because I don't want you getting hurt."

He looked remarkably offended. Like, the most offended I've ever seen someone. *"What?"*

I ignored Karla and Trevor standing up and huddling next to each other, far away from the table, and lit into Xander. "It was one thing to stay with Karla and Trevor when I was going to live in hiding. They were going to relatively safe since I wouldn't exist here. But living out in the open with *you* can bring that psycho to your door, Xander. What don't you get about that?"

He looked murderous. His snarl was low and deep and serious. "I'm going to forget that you just called me a pussy, just like you're going to forget I was an asshole to you when we first met. And with that, you are going to move your shit into my house, and you are going to stay with me until I say it's safe for you not to. Understand?"

My eyes widened as I reared back at his audacity. "You can't do that. Who do you think you are?"

His eyes narrowed. "I'm the bastard who will stay in the motel room next to yours if I have to. You think you're being stalked now, just you wait, Fallon."

"Fuck you!"

"I have no problem doing that for you, too!"

Trevor had me by the waist and Karla was pushing Xander back before I could fully launch myself across the table at the asshole and kill him with my bare hands. "I am not moving in with you!" I screamed like a lunatic.

"Yes, you are!" Xander fired back.

This asshole.

CHAPTER 14

Xander ~

I was pretty sure I was going to have to sleep with one eye open for the rest of my days, but who needed sleep anyway?

After Trevor and Karla had kept Fallon from killing me-and with a *ton* more common sense from Trevor-Fallon had caved and had agreed to move in with me temporarily. She wasn't happy about it, but she'd chosen the not-cutting-off-her-nose-to-spite-her-face route. And now I was at her motel room, picking her up to move her in. I had even let some of the guys knock off work early and that wasn't my norm. Mackley O'Brien-or Mac as we like to call him-had even made a comment about how I must be feeling sick or something.

The asshole.

Little could I admit that it was the something-*or rather, someone*-that had me twisted up in knots, and not that I'd been coming down with the flu.

I knocked on the door, and a few seconds later, it swung open, and a fresh-out-of-the-shower Fallon stood before me. Her face was free of makeup and her dark hair was thrown up in a bun on top of her head, but it looked damp.

Fuck, she was pretty.

Even in a light blue t-shirt, jeans, and plain sandals she looked beautiful.

I glanced behind her and saw her a couple of bags sitting on the bed. "You ready?"

She stepped back and allowed me entrance. "Almost," she answered. "I'm paid up through tomorrow morning, but I let the clerk know that I'd be leaving today."

"Well, since you decided to use your real name to check in, maybe your check out will make it look like you've moved on," I replied before reaching for the bags on the bed. "Is this all of it?"

"Yeah. I just have to officially check out, but I can grab the bags an-"

I shot her a withering look over my shoulder as I grabbed her bags. "We're going to have ourselves a little talk when we get to my place, Fallon."

"Xand-"

"Not now and not here," I said, interrupting her. "But we *are* going to talk." She let out an irritated huff but didn't argue any further.

I hauled her bags to my truck in one trip as she did one final sweep of the motel room. I waited by the passenger door, then I opened the door for her when she finally made her way to the truck. I thought she was going to give me shit for opening the door for her and closing it once she got settled, but she didn't.

Small favors.

The drive to the motel office was a short one, and the defiant little brat had her hand on the door handle and was hopping out of the truck before I had even had it in park. I let out a string of curse words as I watched her disappear into the motel office. I still got out of the truck and went inside to show her that I wasn't going to be so easily dusted off.

After Fallon checked out of her motel room, we repeated our earlier steps where I opened the truck door for her, then she got in without a word. In fact, the entire drive back to my place was in complete silence, but I didn't care. At the end of the day, Fallon was safer with me than she was with Trevor and Karla. It wasn't that they couldn't protect her, but Karla would always be Trevor's first priority-as it should be-and Karla would get his ultimate protection over Fallon. This way, living with me, there was nobody to be torn between. Fallon would get all of me if it came down to it.

I pulled into my driveway and tried to look at my house through Fallon's eyes. It was a single-story home with a functional attic that I used for a workshop. My office was used for the administrative side of my business, but the attic was where I allowed my messes. The shed I was expanding was used to store my bigger machinery, plus my lawnmower and shit like that.

The house was like I had explained to Fallon yesterday. It had three bedrooms, two and a half baths, a kitchen, living room, dining room, and a huge deck that led to my backyard. It could be argued that the house was too big for just one man, but I hoped to fill it with a wife and some kids one day.

I opened the door, and again, Fallon was out of the truck before I could open the door for her. I reached in the back for her bags and had them all hauled up for one trip. Fallon really had traveled lightly, and the bags didn't weigh a thing.

She quietly followed me up the walkway to the front door and waited patiently as I unlocked the door. I stepped back, and taking my life in my own hands, I reached back, placed my hand on the small of her back, and escorted her inside. She hadn't flinched or rushed to get away, so I was going to count it as a win.

I set her bags down in next to the entry wall and pulled her key copy off my key chain. "This is your copy of the house key," I told her, handing it to her. I placed it in her palm and her face conveyed just how uneasy she still was with all of this. "It opens the front door, the back door, and the garage door."

Her blue peepers glanced over at the front door. "And the deadbolts?"

"Those are key-less. They work off a code," I explained.

Her eyes rounded. "Really?"

I smiled softly at her surprise. "Yeah. Really."

"What if I forget the code?"

I grabbed her bags again. "We can reprogram them to something you'll remember if you want. Now let me show you to your room." She followed me without another word.

When we got to her room, I set her bags down on the bed and gave her the rundown. "As you can see, the room's set up like any other bedroom across America. You can use it however you see fit."

There wasn't anything really exciting about the room. The walls were painted a soft grey with dark grey curtains on the window that viewed into the backyard. The bed was a queen with matching dark grey bedding. There was a small closet, but between that and the dresser on the right side of the room, there was plenty of clothing space. The entire bedroom set matched with two nightstands and a hope chest at the foot of the bed. It was simple, but efficient.

The entire house was pretty much set up the same way. Every room looked like it belonged in a showroom, not because I was fancy, but because all the furniture in each room matched itself. The only exception was my bedroom. My bedroom was my sanctuary and my safe place, and where my personality breathed. It was a hodgepodge of personal stuff from my childhood until now. When I'd bought the house, I'd an interior designer that I partnered with a lot on my projects decorate my house, but I'd made it clear that my bedroom was off limits.

"What do you think?"

She blew me away with her manners. I was still feeling guilty about our first meeting and hadn't expected much. Her blue eyes looked into mine. "You have a very nice home, Xander," she said graciously.

Not sure why I suddenly felt heat crawl up my neck, but I did. "Well, I'll let you get settled, and then give you a tour."

I went to turn, but she stopped me. "Xander?"

"Yeah?"

"Uhm, do you...do you have a safe or...something?" she asked nervously.

I cocked my head at her nervousness. I've seen Fallon in a different array of emotions, but not nervous, which was surprising seeing as how she had a crazy person tracking her. "I have a couple of safes along with a lock closet in the attic."

"What's a lock closet?"

"It's just a small room that houses stuff I can't fit into a safe."

"What on earth would you store in there?"

"I have a lot of expensive equipment that I lock up when not in use. Everything I own for my business is debt-free."

She didn't remark on that as I watched different expressions play out on her face in thought. Finally, she asked, "Would it be okay if I stored my bag in one of your safes or your room?"

My brows drew down. "Which bag?"

Fallon grabbed the small, strapped bag from the bed. "This one."

"What's in it?" I remembered Karla had said that Fallon wasn't a fan of guns, but I needed to know if this woman had brought a gun into my home. I had a couple of them locked up in my safe, but they were registered, and I knew how to use them.

Her lips rolled in, and she shrugged a shoulder. "My money," she replied.

What?

"I'm sorry, what?"

"It's my money," she repeated. "Everything I have."

I snatched the bag from her hand, then opening it up, I could see it was filled with cold, hard fucking cash. My eyes flew to hers. "You've been carrying this around with you?" She nodded. "Are you fucking crazy?"

Fallon let out a deep sigh as she dropped on the bed. "Nope," she murmured. "Just exhausted."

Well, fuck.

CHAPTER 15

Fallon ~

It's been almost two months of normal, but I was still realistic enough to know that it was probably too good to be true.

After Xander had lectured me about the thousands I'd been carrying around like cheap luggage, he'd given me a tour of his home and had gone over the rules. Albeit there hadn't been many that didn't fall under basic common courtesy, but he'd been adamant about the fact that he was the man of the household and that meant there'd be doors opened for me, bags carried in for me, and the like. I'd been right when I had pegged Xander Raynes for being a man's man, and he wasn't apologetic about it at all.

I wasn't going to lie, though. Having gone it alone for all these years, it felt nice to have someone around to do all those little things that didn't seem like they mattered enough to make a difference, but they did.

It took me only two weeks to find a job at Cut & Clips, and while not glamorous, it was a job I was grateful for. I was by no means a stylist or beauty guru, but the salon's vibe was energetic enough that I didn't mind sweeping up hair, stocking shelves, or refiling shampoo containers. And since the salon was only open during daylight hours, I had a day shift that made it possible for me to be home safe at night.

I had also managed to find a used car in the sale ads that I'd gotten for cheap. Randall was a high school junior who had wanted to upgrade his car to something a little cooler, so I'd gotten his used KIA for a good bargain.

All in all, everything was coming together, and I felt I was finally in a place where I could start looking for a place of my own. I was finally living a semi-normal life where I wasn't afraid to have a cellphone, bank account, job, and somewhat friends. Being near Karla was also a great plus. We talked all the time and had lunch together at least once a week. It was…nice.

The only dark spot in my rather sunny picture was that Brant was a lot smaller town than I had been prepared for. Living in big cities in California, I hadn't given much to gossip or worried about what my neighbors had been into. Brant was a different animal altogether; mainly, me living with Xander.

One thing that salons were notorious for was gossip and Cut & Clips was full of it. I'd heard more than I wanted to about what a catch Xander Raynes was, and I had to let the gossip fly because I couldn't tell people the real reason that I was living with Xander. Sure, I kept sticking to the script that he was just helping me out as a favor to Karla and Trevor, but nobody bought my story. The town was full of women who believed in Lifetime Original Movies and romantic comedies that they've convinced themselves that I was *living* with Xander. So, the sooner I could move out, the sooner I could squash some of the rumors.

Not to mention, living with Xander was harder than I thought it would be. I learned early on that my living with him had no effect on his daily life. The man walked around in just basketball shorts or sweats all the time. Hell, a few times I caught him in just a towel, fresh out of the shower and, trust me, that wasn't a good thing when the man was shredded all to hell and was sexy as sin. I didn't need my attraction to Xander to deepen. I had real-life problems that didn't include a reformed jackass in my bed.

The surprising thing was that we got along fairly well. I'd been certain that our personalities would clash, but they hadn't yet, and we had fallen into a nice, cordial routine. I even stopped fighting his alpha tendencies and let him be the man of the house. Everything was working out, if only the women at the salon would stop plaguing me with questions about how good the man was in bed.

With the decision to start looking at places to live, I sat at the house computer in Xander's office and pulled up realty listings for Brant, North Dakota. I wasn't sure how long I'd been seated at the computer before I heard Xander's deep, rumbling voice behind me. "What are you doing?"

I looked up, startled and surprised. "What are you doing here?"

He was leaning against the door frame with his arms crossed over his chest. "I live here," he smirked.

I rolled my eyes. "I mean, what are you doing home already?"

"Fallon, it's past six," he said, jerking his head towards the clock on the wall.

I glanced back down towards the corner of the computer screen, and sure enough, it was a little past six already. "Shit," I mumbled. "I hadn't realized it was that late."

"What are you doing?" he asked again.

I looked back up at him. *Damn, the man really was a good-looking sonofabitch.* "I was checking real estate listings for condos or apartments," I replied.

I could see the tick in his jaw. "Why?"

I logged out of the website, then powered down the computer before standing up and walking towards him. "Because now that I've got a car and a job, it's time I find a place to live," I said, leaving the 'duh' out of my answer, but letting it be implied.

"You don't like living here?"

Okay.

I was not expecting that.

"That's not the point," I replied, a might bit confused. "This was a temporary arrangement, or did you forget? The plan was that I'd move out once I got settled, Xander."

Something passed in his eyes and, suddenly, things didn't feel that simple anymore. "You're wrong, Fallon," he said. "The arrangement was that you'd move out once *I* felt it was safe for you to do so."

I was standing in front of him, blown away by his words. "What? What are you talking about?"

"The agreement was that you'd stay here until I felt it was safe enough for you to move out." He straightened as he shrugged a shoulder. "It's only been a few weeks," he pointed out. "I don't feel...uh, comfortable with you moving out just yet."

I stood there not sure what I was feeling. He couldn't be serious, could he?

I shook my head to clear the muddiness his word had created. "You don't have a say, Xander," I replied. "You...it's not up to you, contrary what your alpha man mind may think."

"That was the deal, Fallon," he argued.

I wanted to be a jerk and tell him that he didn't have a say again, but I quickly realized Xander wasn't being a macho alpha. I was pretty sure that he really was concerned about me leaving. Sure, we've been living together for a few weeks, but it wasn't as if we'd become friend-friends. We'd been...easy roommates; nothing more. So, his concern was a little...well, concerning.

"Xander, I...I can't live here forever," I whispered. "The whole point of getting a job and...all this, is to finally meet this situation head-on. I can't do that if I'm living here."

There went that tick in his jaw again. "Why not?"

"Because that's the coward's way out, Xander," I replied. "This is my problem. I need to...deal with it myself."

He looked pissed. "It's not cowardice to accept help from friends."

I didn't want to be a jerk, but I wasn't going to sugarcoat this conversation, either. "Xander, we're hardly friends," I pointed out. "And even if we were, accepting help from a friend is different from putting them in harm's way. Why do you think I don't hang out with Karla as much as I'd like to?"

Xander stepped to me, and a small part of me almost stepped back, but I stood firm and held his gaze. "What are we if we're not friends?" He stuffed his hands in his pockets like they'd be safe there. "For fuck's sake, Fallon, we live together."

"You let me stay with you, Xander," I corrected. "That's not the same as living with someone. And with that, I'd say we're more roommates than we are friends."

"Oh, really?" The irritation was plain as day in his voice.

"Yeah, really," I said with just a little bit of bite. He was being ridiculous. "I can count on one hand what I know about you, Xander. I know your name, what you do for a living, that Trevor is your best friend, and that you're single. Four things, Xander. I know *four* things about you."

He gave me a tight nod, but he looked upset. "Yeah, well, you want to know what I know about you?" He didn't let me answer. "I know your name, what you do for a living, that Karla is your best friend, and that you're single. But I also know that you're not a morning person. You prefer tea to coffee. You're neat and clean up after yourself. You like to read murder mysteries. You can cook, but what you really like to do is bake. I know you have a smile for everyone you meet, even after what you've been through and are going through. I know you hate to wear shoes and prefer to be barefoot or in socks. I also know you'd wear pajama pants all day if the world would let you."

His rant was like a kick to the chest. This entire time, while I've been doing my best to stay out of his way while I got my life on track, Xander's been paying attention.

Paying attention to *me*.

"Xander-"

His hands came out of his pockets, and he reached out to cradle my face. "Go to dinner with me, Fallon," he commanded, instead of asking. "Go to dinner with me tomorrow night."

My answer was going to change everything, but there was only one answer I could give him. This was a *bad* idea, but the word that came out of my mouth was, "Okay."

CHAPTER 16

Xander ~
She'd said yes.

I hadn't really planned on asking Fallon to dinner, but when she had called us roommates, that hadn't sat well with me. For weeks, I've been noticing everything that made up Fallon Reese without suffocating her and giving her room to get her life together, and it stung when she admitted to not knowing anything about me. Here I'd been thinking that I'd been just taking things slow, but she'd made it clear that we hadn't even moved from where we'd been the day that I met her.

And now, we sat across from each other at Dailies, waiting for our orders, and hopefully becoming more than friends.

Because I really wanted to be more than friends with Fallon Reese.

"So, you said you only knew four things about me," I reminded her. "What more do you want to know?"

She didn't pussyfoot, which I appreciated. Life was always easier with a straight shooter. Less confusion that way, more hurt feelings, perhaps, but less confusion. "Let's start with your family," she replied, telling me a lot more about her than I already knew. Most women would want to know about my business and how cozy my savings account was. At least, that's been my experience when trying to date seriously.

"My parents passed a few years ago," I answered, and her face immediately softened. "They died in a car accident."

"I'm sorry," she whispered.

"Thank you," I replied. "The construction company was my father's, and when he died, I came home to take over."

"Were you close?" The question was asked with enough sincerity in her voice that it felt like she was asking because she genuinely wanted to know.

"We were." And we really had been. I'd had great parents. "It's the reason I gave up life in the big city in suits and ties to come back."

She cocked her head to the side. "No regrets?"

I shook my head. "None." And I meant that.

"No siblings?"

"No. My mother had a couple of miscarriages after I was born, and my dad hadn't wanted more children at the risk to my mother's health. So, they had shut down shop and went to just raising me." I leaned forward. "What about you?"

Before Fallon could answer, the waitress came with our meals. Once everything was situated to start eating, she answered, "My parents were killed in a car wreck, too. A drunk driver."

It was something I wasn't expecting, but it was something that connected us. "An inexperienced winter driver is what caused my parents' accident."

Fallon took a bite of her seasoned salmon before asking, "What were their names?"

My lips curved upward. I loved how she was asking for details. "Daniel and Sela Raynes. Yours?"

"Harold and Kimberly Reese," she said, the same wistful smile on her face. "I don't remember much because I was so young when they died, but what I do remember is good."

"And foster care?" I wasn't sure if I should ask the question because foster care could be a tough subject for people who'd fallen into the pitfalls that sometimes came with living in foster care. Still, I wanted to know what made Fallon tick. I'd made the decision to pursue her, and that's what I was doing.

"It could have been worse," she said vaguely. "Being friends with Karla helped a lot."

"How so?"

Between bites, Fallon went on to tell me all about living in foster care. Her story wasn't as dark as it could have been, but it wasn't all sunshine and roses, either. She talked about meeting Karla and some of the other kids that she'd gotten along with. She also talked about how lonely she'd been when Karla had gone to live with her family.

When she was done, she surprised me with another personal question. This one geared more towards my personal, personal life. "No ex-wives?"

I let out a soft laugh. "No. No ex-wives," I replied. "Nor will I ever have one."

Her brows shot up. "Never getting married?"

I made sure to hold her blue gaze as I clarified my statement. "Not that. I just meant that when I do get married, it will be forever. No divorce."

She leaned back in her seat as she regarded me and mulled over my statement. "Shit happens."

"And that's fine. However, it will take a lot to make me walk away from my marriage if I ever have one."

Fallon leaned forward. "What if *she's* the one who wants to walk away?"

I leaned in. "She won't," I vowed. "But in the event that she did want to, there's no way I'd ever let her go without a hell of a fight."

Fallon's words were raspy. "Ever?"

I held her gaze as I told her the truest words I've ever spoken. "Over my dead body, will my wife ever leave me, Fallon."

"Because?" Her voice hitched as she asked the word, and I could tell my possessiveness was turning her on. I imagined it was because, as a foster kid, she's never been wanted or claimed. It was something she probably fantasized about being.

"Because I'll only love once, Fallon," I explained. "I'll only love once, and I'll never do anything that will make my wife want to leave me. Piss her off? Sure. Make her want to murder me? Definitely. But leave me? Never."

I wasn't sure if she meant to say it, but her words sounded genuinely concerning. "Do you think the person who's after me thinks they're in love with me like that?"

Suddenly, I heard my words through her ears, and I needed to clarify. "It's different when you return the love, Fallon. What I'm banking on is that my wife will love me every bit as much as I love her, and she won't want to ever leave me. Even through the hard times, I will be banking everything on her love for me. The guy or girl stalking you isn't in this for love. Love is every bit as freeing as it is confining, and whoever is after you doesn't make you feel free."

"No. No, they don't," she quietly agreed.

She didn't say anything as the waitress brought our check and I didn't push, but she finally looked at me and said, "The possessiveness towards your future wife is rather…comforting."

I snorted out a laugh. "Hope she thinks so," I said wryly. "But it's more likely she'll feel it'll be stifling."

"I hope not," she replied. "There's a real security in knowing you're wanted with such fierceness."

I didn't want to say it, but she was confusing me. I wouldn't think someone who was being stalked would appreciate possessiveness. "But aren't you being wanted with that kind of fierceness right now?"

Fallon gave me a small shake of her head. "No," she replied. "If I was, he would have made his move by now, don't you think?"

I smirked at how she threw my words back at me. "Touché, Ms. Reese." She gave me a soft laugh and a sassy wink, then everything south of my waistband sat up and noticed.

I had wanted to go slow. I had wanted to show her that I wasn't the dick I'd acted like when we first met. I'd wanted her comfortable and I'd wanted her to trust me. I'd wanted her to feel safe before I made my move. However, the more time I spent with her, the more I realized being in my bed was the farthest thing from her mind. Hell, I wasn't even sure if I was on her list of things to do at all.

Still, I knew if I wasn't completely honest, I'd get nowhere with her. She needed blunt honesty because her life was confusing enough as it was. And Fallon might not like me, but she was attracted to me, and I'd use that if I had to in order to push us forward.

"Fallon, can I tell you something without you freaking out?" She blinked at me, and then threw her head back in a genuine laugh. I smiled as she calmed down. Laughter was a good look on her.

After she calmed down, she asked, "Seriously?" My smile widened. "Does that ever work? Telling someone not to freak out only makes them freak out, Xander."

"Point taken," I agreed. "But I still would like to tell you something without you freaking out."

Fallon stopped laughing, but her smile was still in place. "Okay, Raynes, hit me with it."

I leaned in closer, so that the entire eatery couldn't listen in on what I was sure to be one of me least finest moments. Charm and suaveness were absent at this dinner table. "I know you've got a lot going on, and I know sex is probably the furthest thing from your mind, but I want you in my bed, Fallon. I've wanted you in my bed for a while now." The smile slid off her face and I knew I fucked up.

"Uh…"

"I don't need you to start ripping your clothes off or anything, but…but I wanted to know if the attraction is one-sided." *Here was my shot.* "Do you want me, Fallon?"

She didn't answer right away, and I was hit with the unwelcoming sensation that she was probably going to rush home and start packing. But instead, she surprised me by saying, "I probably shouldn't."

That wasn't a no.

CHAPTER 17

The Past ~

I never expected her to leave California.

I expected her to move like she always did, but I never expected her to move damn near across the country.

Brant, North Dakota.

Brant, North Dakota where Karla Dallas was now Karla Graig. Where Fallon Reese had fled to and was now living with a man who had no right to be anywhere near her.

Fallon Reese was mine.

She has always been mine.

She was always meant to be mine.

When her name had flagged in Indiana, and then North Dakota, I knew this wasn't like all the other times. Something changed and I had a feeling the man who was opening the truck door for her was the reason for the change. Not knowing how long they'd be gone, I hadn't had time to find out.

I watched, nestled in the darkness, as they came back from their date, and he got out, walked around, and then helped her out of the truck. I watched as he placed his hand on the small of her back and I noticed how she didn't flinch or shy away from his touch.

I wasn't sure how long she's been living with him, but I knew the second I'd gotten into town that she was staying with him. She had a job, a car, and a bank account on record, but no apartment or house. After staking out the Graigs' residence and seeing no signs of Fallon, I had laid low until I found her walking out of a salon one day, then I followed her to some guy's house. That guy turned out to be one, Xander Raynes.

Xander Raynes.

He was the first man who's intruded on what I had with Fallon. While Fallon has run many times before, she had always run alone. She lived alone and did nothing but wait for my next move. But now, she was living with another man and letting him touch her.

Did he know about me?

Did he know about me, or was she here just trying to make a fresh start? Was she here and pretending that I no longer existed? Was she here trying to pretend that I wouldn't follow her? Did she really believe that she would end up with anyone other than me?

I've been in love with her my whole life. I've been following her, giving her time for the past six years. Did she really believe that I'd let another man come in and take the only thing that has ever mattered to me?

I might have had to share her body, but everything else was mine. I had to let him know that. I had to let *her* know that.

I watched as Xander unlocked the front door to his house and guided Fallon inside, and the need to run in there and claim her as mine was stronger than it's ever been.

She. Was. Mine.

Fallon Reese was mine, and right now, she was probably in that house letting Xander Raynes touch her. Kiss her. Move inside her.

My hands were white-knuckled and the quiet was being invaded with static and chaos. I stuck my right hand in my pocket and circled my fist around the little ceramic rabbit that was always with me. The rabbit that was our connection.

Another thing that we had in common besides that wretched foster home.

Knowing that Xander Raynes was probably making Fallon promises he couldn't keep, I knew I had to finally make my move. I knew I couldn't put it off any longer.

I'd wanted to give her time to come around. I'd wanted to give her time to get used to the idea of how deep my love for her was. I'd wanted her to see that, in the end, the only thing she had in this world was me. But then she ran to someone I hadn't seen coming. It had never occurred to me that she was still friends with Karla Dallas.

She had run to Karla Dallas-or Graig-and with that, she had ended up in the arms of Xander Raynes.

Well, no more.

I was here and there was no going back.

I was here and it was time to show her where she belonged and who she belonged to because it sure as fuck wasn't Xander Raynes.

It was me.

CHAPTER 18

Xander ~

My heart threatened to beat out of my chest with anticipation.

After Fallon hadn't elaborated on her 'I probably shouldn't' comment, I'd grabbed the check, paid the waitress, grabbed Fallon by her hand, then had walked her back out to my truck.

The ride home had been quiet as fuck, but I hadn't wanted to open my mouth and run the risk of saying something stupid enough to make her change her mind about me. Hell, or worse, remind her of the asshole I'd been when we first met.

Shutting the front door behind us, I knew it was now or never. "Fallon-"

She turned around and looked up at me. Her eyes were warm and her expression guileless. "This is a bad idea, Xander," she said, her voice matter of fact.

I stepped to her, and I wished I could say I was surprised by her words, but I wasn't. This *was* a bad idea from her perspective. I reached for her and placed one hand on her back while the other one cradled her face. "I can understand why you'd feel that way, baby." And I could. Her life was changing rapidly, and big decisions were being made without adding this one to it. I also wasn't going to apologize for calling her baby, even with all that surprise on her face. I was in this for real. "I get that…you have a lot going on, and the last thing I want to do is take advantage of your situation, but, Christ, Fallon…I've been patient. I've been living here with you for weeks, staying out of your way, and waiting for you to feel comfortable and…alive. I don't think I can wait anymore." *Not without losing my fucking mind.* "It'd be different if you didn't want me back, but I know you do."

Fallon closed her eyes and the sigh that escaped sounded deep, lonely, and tiring as fuck. However, that was the thing…I wanted to carry her. I knew how exhausted she was, and I wanted to pick up the battle for her. And if not fight it for her completely, at least help her with her fight. While we haven't spoken much on her stalking, I could see the toll it's taken on her, and I couldn't stand it anymore.

She opened her eyes to look at me. "I don't want to use you, Xander."

Her words were like a kick to the chest. I dropped my hands and stepped back. I had called her out on her attraction to me, but attraction didn't equal like. And if she was afraid to use me, then that must mean she didn't like me. She'd just be with me to stave off the loneliness.

Well, that fucking sucked.

"You still don't like me," I said. No accusation. No blame. Just a statement of fact.

Fallon's beautiful blue eyes widened. "What? No. What are you talking about?"

I shrugged a shoulder. "You said that you didn't want to use me. It'd only be using me if you were only invested in sex and nothing more."

She let out another exhausting sigh. "That's not what I meant, Xander."

I jammed my fists in my pockets, doing my best to keep the frustration out of my voice. I wasn't mad, just…I wanted this woman so goddamn badly. "Then what did you mean?"

"I just meant…I could easily get used to living inside this little bubble with you, pretending that it can't just all come to an end at any moment. I don't want to use you as an escape. I…I gotta know that you're really committed to this before we take this any further."

"I am." The words flew out of my mouth without any hesitation.

"Xander, someone is after me," she replied as if I didn't understand English. "Do you get that? I mean, do you *really* get that? You say you want more than sex, but do you really understand what 'more' with me means?"

"No," I told her honestly. "No, I don't. However, I do know that I want you badly enough to go for it without knowing."

She scoffed. "That's hormones, Xander."

I stepped to her and took her face in my hands again. "Bullshit," I snapped. "If it were hormones, I'd be balls-deep in some random female at the bar or somewhere. Instead, I'm here with you. I've been here with you, and *only* you, for weeks, Fallon. Waiting. Praying. Wanting."

"If something happens to you-"

I slammed my mouth down on hers, stopping the words she was going to say to convince herself not to do this with me. My hands slid up into her hair and I deepened the kiss as soon as I heard the deep, rumble of her moan. I might be taking advantage of her attraction to me, but I was beyond doing the gentlemanly thing. If I didn't use everything I could to my advantage, Fallon would never give me a chance. Hell, I wasn't sure if she'd give anyone a chance with what she was going through.

I tore my mouth off her and started tasting her skin. "Xander…" she moaned, and it was like fucking music to my ears. Her hands grabbed at my waist, and it felt like I was on fire.

"I'm going to taste every inch of your skin, baby," I promised between nips and kisses on her neck.

Fallon started pulling at my belt and her words sounded as desperate as I felt. "Later," she whimpered. "You can kiss me all over later, Xander. Right now, I need you."

I pulled back to look at her face. Her eyes were clouded over, and her face was flushed, and I hadn't even done anything yet. It made me feel like a goddamn king. "Fallon, I don't want to just take you. I want to worship the fuck out of you."

"This first time, take me, Xander," she begged. "You can worship me later. I promise." Then she hit me with honesty I couldn't deny her. "It's been so long."

"Fallon, you're killing me," I breathed against her neck.

She pulled back and looked up at me. "I…" Her eyes glossed over, and in that moment, I knew I couldn't be that guy.

"We don't have to do-"

"No," she rushed out. "I just…I feel *desperate*, Xander." She sounded desperate. "I feel…I think I'll go crazy if you take your time. I'm feeling too many things all at once and I feel like I'm going to explode if you don't…if you don't make it all go away."

Well, hell.

I grabbed her face and made sure she was looking me in the eye when I asked, "Are you sure you want to do this? There's no going back, Fallon. No running away afterwards."

Instead of answering me, Fallon reached for my jeans again and I followed her lead. I wasn't going to overthink it, and if I was taking advantage of her, so be it. It wasn't like I was going to kick her out of my bed as soon as I nutted anyway. If she felt vulnerable afterwards, I planned on being there to make it all better.

Clothes were being discarded, shoes kicked off, bodies attacked and, suddenly, romance didn't sound as appealing at it had earlier. I wanted Fallon. I've *been* wanting her. The only rub was that I wasn't entirely sure she wanted me or just any guy to stave off the loneliness, but I was going to do my best to make sure it was me that she wanted when this was all said and done.

Naked and ready, I grabbed Fallon by the back of her thighs, and she was already onboard with wrapping her legs around my waist. I walked us towards the nearest wall and as soon as her back made contact, I let the wall bear her weight and I slid the head of my dick through the wet folds of her pussy. She might not want romance, but I was still going to make sure I didn't rip her open. I had to test how ready she was for me before sliding home, and if the slick sounds mixed with our harsh breaths were any indication, Fallon was ready for me.

However, I still felt the need to warn her. "This might hurt, baby," I said against her ear.

"I don't care," she moaned. "I just want you."

I closed my eyes for one brief second, praying I wasn't ruining everything, and then slammed into her wet, willing body, causing Fallon to throw her head back in a scream that I felt all the way to my bones. And, Christ, she felt every bit as addicting as I knew she would. Her pussy was the hottest and tightest thing to ever touch my dick.

I stayed buried to the hilt inside her, giving her a moment to get accustomed to my size. Her nails were digging into my shoulders, and I secretly hoped she drew blood. I needed this woman dependent on my cock. I needed her to need me every fucking day. "You okay?"

Her breaths were harsh, and I knew she was uncomfortable, if not hurting. "Yes," she lied. "Move, Xander. Please, just move…"

So, I did.

I grabbed her hips and I pulled out before slamming back into her with the same force and intensity as the first time. I hoped what she meant about not wanting romance because this was not romantic at all.

This was animalistic.

I fucked my cock into her tight cunt like she had no choice. I rammed my cock into her as far as it could go, and I didn't let up, no matter how loud my legs were screaming. My fingers were deep in her hips and her back was going to be bruised with the force of every crash against the wall. And all the while, she was begging me for more, and she was doing it using my name.

She was calling out *my* name.

"I'm cumming, Xander," she cried, and I fucked her through every tremor and every ripple. Not five minutes later, I followed as I emptied everything I had inside her precious body.

CHAPTER 19

Fallon ~

Wow.

Now, granted, it's been a long time since I've been with a man, but Xander had not disappointed last night.

Still laying in his bed, feeling his warmth against my back, I knew it wasn't loneliness that had drawn me to Xander so much as it was that I was tired. I was so tired from fighting all this darkness alone. Sure, it wasn't fair to him, but he kept assuring me that he was in this with his eyes wide open. And if that were the case, then I had to trust that he meant what he said. He was willing to see where this went, even if it became difficult. It also didn't hurt that he knew what he was doing in the bedroom. And in the shower. And up against the wall.

Last night had been great as far as nights of sex went. After I'd begged him to put the romance on hold, he'd brought it out the second time he had slid inside me. Once we'd made it to the bed, Xander had savored every part of my body with his lips, tongue, and hands. He had studied me like he'd been cramming for finals, and the man's final grade was an A+++. I was still concerned about this moving too fast, but I was going to trust in what I was feeling.

And I was feeling a lot of things.

However, right now, I was feeling the need to pee, so I started to roll out of Xander's embrace, but he wasn't as asleep as I thought he was. "Where you going?" he mumbled against the back of my neck as his arm tightened around my waist.

"I need to use the restroom."

"Well, I suppose if you *have* to," he teased, but released me, so I could get out of his bed. Last night, he had carried me to his bedroom and that's where we had stayed. I wasn't sure what the protocol was now that we'd slept together, but Xander struck me as the type of man who will have my stuff moved into his bedroom by the end of the day.

I sat up, and completely naked, got out of bed. I wasn't a huge fan of parading around without any clothes on, but Xander had kissed damn near every inch of my skin last night, so it seemed rather juvenile to be bothered by my nudity now. Not to mention, I could also grab a robe or some pajamas from my room while I freshened up.

Xander stopped me as I headed towards the bedroom door. "Hey, where are you going?"

I turned my head to look back at him. "I told you. I'm going to the restroom."

His sleepy face looked confused. He pointed towards his adjoining bathroom door. "Use that one," he directed.

I rolled my eyes. "Xander, I'd also like to brush my teeth and wash my face."

He rolled those beautiful golden eyes at me back. "Women," he muttered, but he muttered it with a grin on his lips. "Yeah, well, bring your toothbrush back with you and put it in this bathroom.

See? I knew it.

I wasn't opposed to the idea of fully living with Xander, but I didn't want to presume. "Just grab an extra one for in here if it matters to you that much," I replied, testing what this was.

He narrowed his eyes at me. "You're out of your mind if you think you won't be moved into my bedroom by the end of the weekend, Fallon," he growled.

I laughed, then walked out of the room. My bladder was screaming, and I really needed to brush my teeth and wash my face. It wasn't a vanity thing; it was a cleanliness thing. Plus, it gave him time to face the day, too, if he chose. The truth was that Xander Raynes was so hot that morning breath wouldn't be a factor.

After taking care of business, I grabbed some underwear and a t-shirt, threw them on, and then headed for the kitchen. Xander may have done most of the work last night, but I was feeling it everywhere and that made me feel exhausted. Had it not been for my bladder, I probably could have slept a good couple of more hours.

I started the pot for a cup of tea while also making some coffee for Xander. Even though he thought I hadn't been paying attention, I had noticed that little things that he did throughout his day. Coffee-*strong coffee*-first thing in the morning was one of those things.

I toyed with making some breakfast, but the desire to crawl back in bed with Xander was stronger than my growling stomach. I knew we'd have to eat soon or later, but the comfort of Xander and his bed felt more needed than sustenance right now.

Besides, if anything could make me forget I was hungry, it was Xander and the skills he unleashed last night. Xander Raynes was a beast in bed.

Xander liked his coffee black, so after testing the strength of my tea, I grabbed both mugs and headed back towards Xander's bedroom or...well, I wasn't sure. Maybe he was serious, and it would be our bedroom by the end of the day. I wasn't sure. I just knew I liked the sound of that.

Out of habit, I glanced at the wall shelf that hung on the left side of the hallway that led to the bedrooms, and just like that, my world came crashing down once again.

When I had moved in with Xander, I had placed my rabbit on the dresser in the bedroom he had assigned me, but Xander had been kind enough to order me an identical one, and he had placed it on the wall shelf in his hallway. He thought having more than one rabbit would help make me feel safer, and it had.

Until now.

Everything happened in slow motion as my body went into its familiar state of panic.

The rabbit had been moved.

The accustomed sensation of blood thrumming in my ears blocked out the sound of crashing ceramic on the tile floor of the kitchen. Panic blocked out the sensation of hot, scalding tea and coffee splashing against my feet, ankles, and legs. Fear blocked out the sound of my name being yelled from somewhere in the house.

I'd been found again.

But this time, it had only taken a matter of a couple of months. He's never moved this fast before. Whoever was doing this usually waiting until I was settled; comfortable. Well...as comfortable as I could ever be.

I sensed movement all around me, but my eyes couldn't tear themselves away from that goddamn rabbit. It wasn't until I felt Xander's hands on my shoulders that I snapped out of my fearful trance.

"Fallon!" he yelled with a shake of my shoulders. I blinked and looked into his worried face. Whatever he saw there, it caused his shoulders to sag. "Baby..." he whispered.

"Did you move the rabbit?" That was all that mattered. That was the only question that needed to be asked.

"What?" His brow drew down. "No. Fallon, I need to look at your feet and legs, baby. They're turning red."

I reared back, hurt, confused, scared, and...unhinged. "Who cares about my legs, Xander?! Did you move the fucking rabbit?!"

"No!" he yelled back. "Why in the fuck would I move either of the rabbits?!"

Breathe.

Dawning raced across Xander's face. "Fallon," he said sternly, as if he knew I was about to crack, "I need you check your legs. Let me check your legs then...then we'll check the rabbits, okay?"

I shook my head.

Fuck. My. Legs.

That was until I took a step and heat radiated all over my lower extremities. "Fuck," I hissed.

Fed up, Xander grabbed my hips, lifted me, then placed me on the kitchen island. He went to go…well, I wasn't sure where, but I grabbed his arm. When he turned towards me, I could see the worry in every part of his face. "Check the rabbits, Xander," I begged. *"Please."*

I could tell he didn't want to leave me, but I was two seconds away from full-blown hysteria and I think he knew it. "Okay," he agreed. "I'll go check your room and then…the one on the shelf." His hands came up to cradle my face. "But promise me you're going to stay put. Your legs are bad off. Do not walk on them until I've taken a look, okay?" I could only nod, but that was all it took for Xander to sprint down the hallway.

I sat on the counter, on the verge of losing my shit, as Xander checked my room. How did he get into Xander's house? I knew there was a huge chance he would finally find me once I made the decision to use my real name here in Brant, but how in the hell did he get into Xander's house?

Getting past Xander's security system seemed to confirm that whoever this person was, he or she was good with computers. It would explain always finding me. It would explain getting inside Xander's house. His deadbolts only engaged from the inside of the house. They protected us if we were home, but they did not do a damn thing if we weren't.

I watched as Xander came back down the hallway and stop at the wall shelf. He was so tall that he didn't need to get on his tiptoes to inspect the shelf. When Xander had put the rabbit there, he had sprinkled a thin layer of vacuum dust on it, so we'd know.

And by the defeat in his stance, I'd say we knew.

CHAPTER 20

Xander ~

The rabbit *had* been moved.

The one in the bedroom was still untouched, but the one in the hallway had been moved. And as much as I knew that was Fallon's greatest concern right now, her legs were mine.

I turned towards her. "I'm going to go get the First-"

"Have the rabbits been moved, Xander?" she asked again, not one bit concerned about possible burns on her feet and legs.

I did my best to measure my tone. I didn't want to alarm or upset her. "The one in the bedroom hasn't been moved, Fal-"

"But that one has, hasn't it?"

"Let me get the First-Aid kit, and...and then hear me out, okay?"

"Xand-"

"Fallon, baby, *please,*" I begged. Yes, I was worried about her mental well-being, but I also needed to see to her physically.

She gave me a small nod of her head, then I raced towards upstairs to the attic where I had my industrial First-Aid kit, not caring about the shards of ceramic on the floor. I did a lot of my physical work up there, so that's where I had it. The kitchen and both bathrooms had standard First-Aid kits, but her legs were going to need burn salve and maybe some bandages.

I grabbed the First-Aid kit and was back in the kitchen in record time. I dropped down to inspect her feet and legs, and upon a clearer inspection, it looked like some salve was enough to do the trick. Her skin wasn't blistering, so the burns hadn't been scalding. "I think some salve-"

"Xander."

That was it.

Just my name.

Just my name said in a tone that I knew she wasn't fucking around anymore. Fallon was no longer in the mood to indulge me. Her fear was giving way to anger, and I was fairly sure the anger was at me.

I began to apply the salve to the reddened splotches on her feet and legs. I'd prefer to wash her legs off with a cool, wet towel, but I didn't have the time. Fallon wanted answers and she wanted them now.

"It was moved, but...hear me out." I looked up at her from where I was on my haunches, tending to her legs. "It's possible we could have done it, Fallon."

Her eyes blazed, clearly offended, and on the defensive. "I would *never* move either of those rabbits," she spat. "What are you talking about? Did *you* fucking move it?"

I stood up and looked into her furious face. "No," I bit out. "I didn't move it."

"Well, I sure as hell didn't," she insisted again.

"Sonofabitch, Fallon," I swore. "When we got home last night, you begged me to fuck you up against the wall with everything I had. And I did. It *is* quite possible that we shook the walls enough to move around some of the things that are hanging there."

Her hand shot out as she pointed towards the wall where I had taken her. "You fucked me over there, Xander," she pointed out, but not after making me question everything I'd been proud of last night. "Do you honestly think your skills were so explosive that they shook that wall way over there?"

Well, fuck me. Ouch.

"It's possible," I snarled at her. I mean, I knew there were dicks in the world bigger than mine, but...fuck.

"Was there anything else on the shelf that...*shifted?*" she asked, and her voice told me everything I needed to know. She was still scared, but now she was pissed, thinking I didn't believe her. However, it wasn't that I didn't believe her. I just wanted to explore all other possibilities before zooming in on the worst one.

I walked over to the shelf, and making sure not to touch anything, I looked over the miniature potted plant and picture frame of my parents on the shelf and saw that they hadn't been moved. In that moment, I knew Fallon's concerns were valid.

Her fear was justified.

I turned to face her, and it amazed me how difficult it was to say the words that would bring her entire world crashing down again. We knew this was a possibility. We knew it'd be easy for him to find her as soon as she had started putting down roots in Brant. We'd known this.

We. Had. Known. This.

"Fallon, I need you to list-"

"It's just the rabbit, isn't it?" she asked, though she knew the answer already. I was certain it was written all over my face.

I walked back towards her on the counter until I was standing in between her legs. I cradled her face in my hands. "I'm not going to let anything happen to you, Fallon."

"How did he get into your house, Xander?" she asked, and even though I knew she didn't mean to, it made me feel like shit. I had promised to protect her, and yet it was possible that someone's been in my house. I never had the needs for cameras because...well, this was fucking Brant; crime was minimal. However, looking back, I should have had them installed the second Fallon had agreed to move in with me.

Arrogance was a motherfucker.

"Baby, I don't know," I told her honestly. "But I'm going to go throw some clothes on, then we can go to the store and buy some cameras. I'll install them immediately." I had thrown on some sweats after I had pissed and brushed my teeth because the crashing of the coffee mugs had caused me to run out of the room half dressed. "Let's get dressed, Fallon."

"No," she whispered, and I was sure I heard her wrong.

"What?"

"I said no," she repeated.

"Why the fuck not?" I was getting whiplash here. She was scared, but she didn't want me to buy any cameras. What the hell?

Fallon shook her head, dislodging my hands, then jumped off the counter. I didn't miss her wince as her feet made contact, but she didn't complain about the sensitivity. Tomorrow her feet were going to be more tender and that was going to suck.

She looked up at me and fucked me up further by stating what had been running through my mind, not minutes before. "This was expected, right? We knew there was a chance he'd come after me. Cameras don't help, Xander," she said. "Or, at least, they haven't helped in the past."

"That doesn't mean we shouldn't get them," I argued. "They're good to have for a million different reasons, Fallon."

Fallon reached out and wrapped her fingers inside the waistband of my sweats. It was an oddly intimate thing to do. It was something couples did, and even though we slept together last night, I hadn't expected her to become so comfortable and affectionate so quickly.

"Xander, I'm tired," she replied, her lips trembling, but her voice was tired sounding as fuck. "I'm scared, but, *God*, am I tired."

"Fallon, I...know we agreed that...I knew why you chose to stay and make a life here. I knew that you were ready to stop running, but..." Christ, I wasn't ready. Even if she was ready to stop running, I wasn't ready to face this so quickly. "Fallon, baby, *I* need the cameras," I told her honestly. "There's no way I'll be able to go to work on Monday knowing he's here."

"Cameras don't help, Xander," she repeated.

"Well, then let me call the police," I replied. "If nothing else, they can be on the lookout for strangers new to town."

"Why don't we-"

The sound of shattering glass had me racing towards the back of the house. I looked back over my shoulder and yelled, "Get in the fucking attic now, Fallon!"

"Xander-"

"Get in the goddamn attic *now!*" I needed her safe, but when I heard another window shatter, it turned me back down the hallway towards the kitchen and Fallon racing down the hallway towards the attic access. The attic was the safest place she could be.

When I didn't see anything or anyone near the kitchen, I decided to follow Fallon into the attic to get one of my guns. Both of us being half dressed, I knew Fallon didn't have her phone on her, so I raced towards the bedroom to grab my phone before heading to the attic. We needed to call 911, and this was the first time I've ever cursed not having a landline.

Racing out of the bedroom I came to an immediate halt when I was faced with a man at the end of the hallway, a gun pointed straight at me, and I knew he hadn't shattered one of the kitchen windows. He had shattered one of the glass panes on the door leading to the backyard.

Now, I knew that my security alarm had been set off, but would the police get here before he killed me and Fallon?

That was the question.

CHAPTER 21

Fallon ~

Hiding out in the attic like a coward was not how this should be going down. I should be wherever Xander was. I should be the one facing this thing head-on, not him. I didn't even know the combinations to his safes, so that I could grab a gun.

"Faaaaallon," came a faint voice underneath my feet.

"Don't come out, Fallon!" Xander yelled, and I dropped to my knees. There was only one reason why Xander would be calling out to me, instead of being up here with me.

"Faaaaallon," came that voice again.

Watching movies, I always used to wonder who was right in situations like this. Was the man right for trying to protect the girl, or was the girl right to try to save the man? A man's protective instincts were vicious, but a woman's love was fearless. Besides, this was *my* mess. Even though Xander had walked into this with his eyes wide open, I wasn't going to let him go down alone. He might hate me. He might see me die. He might even strangle me his-damn-self.

However, he'll never doubt what I feel for him.

Was it love? Not sure, but I knew whatever it was, it was enough to make me drop the stairs from the attic.

As soon as the latch sounded, Xander's rage was unmistakable. "Fallon! What the fuck are you doing?!"

I couldn't answer him. Professing my willingness to die for him was probably not a good move in front of someone who had a vast interest in me. Xander might die anyway, but I was going to do everything I could to keep that from happening. Even if that meant leaving with whoever was down there with Xander.

I descended the steps, ignoring Xander's curses, then made my way towards the living room. Every step was taken with fear and resignation. I was terrified, but I also knew I couldn't live like this anymore. This person has taken six years of my life from me, and finally finding some happiness in Brant with Karla nearby and Xander as a possible future, I couldn't let him take anymore. I didn't want to die, but I wanted to live.

Actually live.

Two steps into the living room, I saw Thomas Fischer. It's been ten years, but there was no mistaking that man who had a gun pointing at Xander was Thomas Fischer. He looked exactly as I remembered, just older and healthier.

Thomas had always been a bright kid, and had he not been a poor foster kid, he'd been the type of boy who would have run with the popular kids. Thomas had always been a good-looking sonofabitch, and he had just grown into a good-looking man. He had light brown hair that paired with a stunning set of hazel eyes that always seemed to look right through you. However, he had been a little on the scrawny side because, half the time, we'd barely been fed enough to keep us alive. However, looking at him now, he had filled out and was nearly as tall as Xander at a little over six-foot.

We'd been friends back then, but that was all.

I ignored a pissed off Xander and focused all my attention on Thomas. "Thomas, what are you doing?"

He didn't answer right away. Instead, his eyes roamed over every inch of me. It reminded me that I was only dressed in a t-shirt and a pair of panties. The shirt came down pass my hips, but not by much. Thomas was getting an eyeful without a bra or pants on. I didn't dare look at Xander because he was probably noticing the same thing.

"Fallon…" My name came out of his mouth like a prayer. It spoke of both reverence and insanity.

"Thomas, what are you doing?" I repeated. "Put the gun down." It never worked in the movies, and I suspected it wouldn't work now, but I had to try something-*anything.*

He shook his head. "It wasn't supposed to happen like this," he replied. "You were supposed to wait for me."

Okay.

He was talking, and that was a good thing. It meant I could buy some time until the police got here. Xander's alarm had surely tripped with the broken windows.

"Wait for you to do what, Thomas?" I took a step closer, and it was enough to set Xander off.

"Stay where the fuck you are, Fallon," he growled.

"Don't talk to her like that!" Thomas roared. "You don't get to talk to her like that!"

I needed to regain Thomas's attention. "Thomas?" He looked over at me again. "W…wait for you to do what?"

"You were supposed to wait for me for when I was ready," he said vaguely, telling me nothing.

"Why don't you let Xander go, and…and we can talk about-"

"The fuck I'm leaving, Fallon," Xander spat, not helping the situation *at all*. I understood that he was upset and scared for me, but Thomas hadn't shot him yet, and I was trying to prevent that.

"If you don't shut the fuck up, I will put a bullet in your head," Thomas seethed. "Don't think I won't." He pushed the tip of his gun against the side of Xander's head. "I should shoot you for touching what's fucking mine anyway."

Xander turned until the gun was pressed up against the center of his forehead. "Then do it," he challenged. "Because the only way Fallon is leaving with you is *over my dead body.*"

"Xander!"

I didn't think.

I ran towards them and stepped in between the two men until Thomas had to pull back or point the gun in my face.

"Are you fucking crazy?" Xander grabbed me, then threw me behind him.

I didn't let him have his way, though. As soon as he released me to face Thomas again, I stepped up from behind him until I was practically standing next to Thomas. "Thomas?"

He looked at me and his eyes were wild and hurt. "You'd die for him?"

"Thomas, the police-"

He threw his head back and laughed. When he looked back down at me, the hurt was gone, but the wild was still there. "The police aren't coming, Fallon," he said. "Our childhood might have been shit, but I've spent the past ten years becoming one of the best hackers in the country. How do you think I'm always able to find you?" I figured as much. Both Karla and I had. It explained everything. "The alarm's been disabled."

"Why are you doing this, Thomas? I thought we'd been friends." It was in that one sentence that I realized I messed up.

"We were?" he disputed.

"I…I thought we had been," I replied, scared of where this might go.

Those stunning eyes of his narrowed. "Then why did you never look back after you left?"

Thomas was a year younger than I was, and he was right. When I had turned eighteen and left foster care, I had never reached out to anyone other than Karla. I'd been so busy trying to get my life together, and putting all those years of rejection behind me, that I hadn't considered the other friends I had left behind.

I thought of feeding him some fairy tale in hopes of calming him, but I couldn't risk him going off on Xander. Plus, he was right. I'd been an asshole. "Thomas, I'm sorry," I told him truthfully. "I was so wrapped up in trying to get my life together that I hadn't thought to reach out to you, or Bonnie, or Samuel, or…well, anyone, really."

"Fuck that shit," Xander barked. "Why the fuck have you been terrorizing her all these years?"

With the gun pointed at Xander this entire time, Thomas looked over at him. "I wasn't terrorizing her," he denied. "I was…waiting until I wasn't mad at her anymore before approaching her."

With men, it really all came down to the basics. "Well, you waited too long," Xander snapped. "Fallon's mine."

I turned to face him. "Xander!" *Why in the hell was he trying to antagonize Thomas?*

"She can't belong to you if you're dead, Xander Raynes," Thomas pointed out.

I turned back towards Thomas. "Thomas, don't…let's calm down," I practically begged. "Let's just…calm down a bit."

He cocked his head at my suggestion. "Does calming down a bit turn this outcome in my favor, Fallon?" he asked rhetorically. "You know, I knew you were going to hit the ground running when you turned eighteen. I could see your determination. You were shy and quiet, but you were strong. You had a quiet strength that wasn't going to hold you down. It's why I took your rabbit. It's all I was going to have left of you when you left."

"You took when I was sixteen, though," I pointed out. We'd been housed in foster care together since I was thirteen, he could have taken it sooner.

"I hadn't known I was going to need it until I overheard you on the phone with Karla, telling her how you were going to beat feet the second you turned eighteen." He sighed. "I needed to keep a piece of you."

And he's been taking pieces of me ever since.

CHAPTER 22

Thomas ~

This was not how I imagined it happening. I hadn't planned on having to murder anyone, but I'll do it if I have to. I didn't come this far, and devote years of my life to Fallon, all for her to end up with someone else.

I also wasn't stupid, though. I knew she was trying to coax me into talking to try to buy some time until she could figure out what to do or talk me down.

Newsflash: There was no talking me down.

"Thomas, I'm sorry if I-"

I shook my head at her. "I don't want to hear your apologies, Fallon," I told her honestly. "Apologies don't garner results. I'm no longer that seventeen-year-old boy who misses you." I kept the gun pointed towards Xander, but I stepped towards Fallon. "I don't think you fully understand what is going on here."

Her composure slipped a bit. "You have a gun on someone," she spat. "Of course, I understand what is going on here."

God, she was so fucking beautiful.

Even as kids, she just radiated beauty. It didn't matter if she'd been dressed in hand-me-downs or that she never wore makeup; Fallon Reese was stunning.

"The day you left, I did what I should have always done, Fallon," I began. "I put my intelligence to use." I had always had a high level of smarts. It had been one of the things that had labeled me as weird. However, no one had known just how smart I really was. "I spent years becoming one of the best IT techs around. Also, I ended up becoming one of the best hackers in the nation. Once I perfected my craft, I searched for you. And I always found you."

She ran her hands through her soft, luscious locks. "But why? Why not just...approach me? Why play games, Thomas?"

Was she for real?

I couldn't help the curl in my lip. "Are you fucking kidding me?" I snarled. "You left me without a backward glance, Fallon. Why would I think you'd meet up with me if I had asked?"

"If you're so smart, you have to know this is not going to work out the way you want," Xander said, the man having no regard for the fact that I had a gun pointed at his face.

My eyes didn't stray from Fallon's as I said, "She ends up with me, or she ends up with no one."

"Thomas, I…"

She trailed off, but I knew it was because she couldn't bring herself to utter the words that she knew would end Xander's life. Fallon wasn't going to go with me voluntarily. She probably believed herself in love with Xander. Still, that didn't matter. While I'd like to have her love, I didn't need it. I just needed *her.*

I stepped towards Xander and pressed the mouth of the gun against the side of his head. "Do I kill him, Fallon?" I asked. "Do I really have leave here with you over his dead body?"

Fallon finally cracked.

Tears started streaming down her face as she whispered in complete anguish, "No."

"Yes," Xander growled at the same time.

"Xander-"

"I'm not letting him leave here with you, Fallon," he snapped. "The *only* way you're leaving here is with me dead."

The exchange of sacrifices should anger me, or at the very least, disgust me, but it didn't. I got it. I was willing to kill for a chance to have a woman like Fallon in my life, so it was completely reasonable for a man to be willing to die for her as well. If I were in Xander's shoes, I'd probably be kissing my life goodbye right now, too. In all actuality, knowing that he's slept with her, Xander should be happy to be leaving this world having experienced what it felt like to exist inside Fallon Reese.

Fallon's face was pure beautiful agony as she begged, "Don't kill him, Thomas. I'll…I'll go with you. I'll do whatever you want." I smiled, ready to bask in my win when the unprecedented happened.

I hadn't counted on Xander initiating the inevitable.

The impact of his right arm coming up, and knocking my arm back, set in motion a fight for our lives when Xander landed a punch with his left into my ribs, causing the gun to fly out of my hand. I heard screaming, but Fallon's lyrical pain was a distant observation. Xander Raynes wasn't fucking around.

But then, neither was I.

After recovering from the blindside, I went at him with everything I had. I tackled him, and we both went flying over the back of the couch. Punches were being landed by both of us, which was expected since we both knew what was at stake here.

Fallon.

The man who won would win her and I refused to be the loser in this. I've been in love with Fallon Reese long before Xander Raynes even knew she existed. Fallon and I shared a childhood together. Xander would never know her the way I did.

The grappling was life or death, and while Xander landed some fierce blows, I had love on my side. A love that even Fallon would never be able to comprehend. "She's mine," I grunted as I took another blow to my stomach.

"Never," Xander swore through bloody teeth. "You'll never have her."

The blows didn't let up and Fallon's crying symphony rang in my ears as I fought Xander with everything I had. The hits were vicious, but then that's what men have been doing since the beginning of time; fighting for that *one* woman who they couldn't live without.

I ignored the blood. I ignored the pain. I ignored the destruction of furniture under my body. I ignored everything that could distract me from winning this fight.

Glass shattered as I slammed Xander against one of the windows and I knew the noise would bring someone running. Sure, I had disabled the alarm system, but I hadn't counted on a full-on brawl that would disturb the neighbors, so it was now or never.

Xander rushed me, unconcerned with the glass shards or the blood, and we landed hard on the floor. It also gave him the advantage of lording over me. While I wasn't a delicate flower, Xander Raynes was fit and strong.

I could still hear Fallon's cries, but that was good. It meant she hadn't run off to call the police. It meant that she was still going to be here when I finished Xander off.

My teeth rattled in my mouth as Xander landed a blow across my jaw. I swung back and landed my mark. "You'll never love her the way I do," I growled.

"Maybe," he snarled as he tried his best to keep the upper hand. "But she'll never love you the way you love her. She'll never love you because she loves *me.*"

And that was all it took.

That one sentence that suggested he's won.

I let out a roar and swung until he was thrown back by the force of my fists. "She's mine!" I screamed as insanity cloaked me in everything that was Fallon Reese. *"She's mine!"*

We were facing each other in a stand to end one another when the unmistakable sound of a gun being cocked vibrated through the room. Over our heaving breaths, over Fallon's tears, over the rush of blood swimming in our ears…over *everything* was that one unmistakable sound.

"Stop!" Fallon shrieked. "Stop!"

Xander and I faced off, but neither of us moved. I wasn't entirely sure

Fallon wouldn't shoot me, and I suspected Xander was afraid she might accidentally shoot him. It was one thing to die for Fallon, it was another to be accidentally shot by her. Both Xander and I wanted to walk out of here with her. Being dead wouldn't help either of us.

Xander finally turned to look at her, and when he did, I turned as well. "Fallon, baby…"

Her face was blotched with tears and pale with fear. Her beautiful blue eyes were round with misery, and I knew she could very well shoot us both unintentionally in her frenzied state. Still, like I said, I wasn't afraid to die for her, but to be killed accidentally, gaining nothing, well…I wasn't onboard with that.

"I called the police," she announced, her voice watery with panic. "I…I called them."

Xander had his hands up in a surrendering motion as he tried to calm her. "Fallon, put the gun down," he instructed through painful, labored breaths. He was trying to defuse the situation, but I also noticed how he didn't instruct Fallon to hand him the gun. He knew-just like I did-that she shouldn't be holding a gun, even if it was to save his sorry ass.

I studied the mess she was, but even with the unrealness of our situation, there was no denying the beautiful spell she had me under. Most of my life, Fallon's been the only beauty in a picture of despair and hopelessness. Maybe if I were a better person, I'd let her go. However, I wasn't, and there was no question if whether I could live without her or not. People threw that phrase around like it didn't hold real meaning, but I couldn't live without a connection to Fallon. She was leaving here with me.

Period.

"Fallon, are you really ready to kill a man?" I asked. "Because that's what you're going to have to do to keep me from getting to you." It was the truth. The police were *not* going to take me away from her. "Because that's the only way this ends."

CHAPTER 23

Fallon ~

The gun shook in my hands.

Through the tears, adrenaline, and fear, the unsteady hold of the gun in my hand was fact. I'd never held a gun before, and I sure as hell have never pointed one at anyone. And for all that he's put me through, I didn't want to shoot Thomas. Maybe if he'd been some random stranger, but knowing who he was, I couldn't live with that on my conscience. Besides, the police were on their way.

I hadn't expected Xander to start a fight, and after getting over the initial shock of it all, I had raced towards the bedroom, grabbed my phone, then dialed 911. I had screamed Xander's address into the phone, and then threw it on the bed while still connected. There was no way I was going to answer some dispatcher's stupid questions while Xander could still be in danger. No matter the fact that Xander and Thomas were equally matched, there'd still been a gun accessible to Thomas.

I had run back out into the living room and had looked for that fucking gun. As soon as I'd seen it, I had raced for it and the relief had nearly brought me to my knees. And while I had no business holding a gun in the state I was in, there was no way I was giving it up until the police got here. At least, that was the plan until Thomas uttered those words that terrified me to the core.

I didn't want to shoot him.

"Thomas, please," I begged. "We...we can..." I didn't know what we could do. I knew he needed to go to jail. I knew he should be punished for everything he's done to me and for threatening to kill Xander, but I was being assaulted with memory, after memory, after memory of the sweet boy who had been so nice to me during those ugly, early years. Thomas was going to go to jail, and I felt wretched that the very idea bothered me.

"I love you, Fallon," he said, matter of fact. "I've always loved you. You're going to have to kill me for that to cease. Nothing matters outside what I feel for you."

"Fallon," Xander's voice broke through Thomas's declaration of love. I turned to look at him. "If you're not going to put the gun down, go outside and wait for the police." He gave me a soft nod. "Put the gun on the ground and wait for the cops."

Did he not understand?

"I'm not letting him out of my sight," I bit out. "I-"

"Fallon," Xander snapped, "if the police come in here with you holding a gun on us, they are going to go after you. Go outside or put the motherfucking gun down!"

Movement on my left had me switching my attention from Xander to Thomas. As a testament to his insanity, he was smirking at me. "Yeah, Fallon," he taunted. "Listen to Xander. Put the gun down."

"Ignore him, Fallon," Xander instructed. "He won't get to you. I won't let him. I swear it, baby."

I could feel my arms trembling and I knew with every passing second, I was putting us all in danger, but I didn't know how to put the gun down. The unknown had me terrified. Intellectually, I knew Xander was right, but emotionally, I couldn't put the gun down.

Was this shock? What this fear paralysis?

I heard the sirens and the sound set off a chain of events I had been hoping to avoid. My knees weakened, and in my fall, Xander rushed towards me and that gave Thomas the opportunity he needed to come at Xander from behind.

"Xander!" I screamed, but not fast enough. Xander took a blow to the side of his head, and the gun fell out of my hands as I instinctively reached for him. I was officially that stupid woman who gave into the emotion of the situation and put both me and Xander in danger again.

Before I could get my bearings, Thomas grabbed my arm, and now it was me standing next to him with a gun to my head. However, the only thing my mind was processing was that there was no way Thomas was getting out of here with me alive. There was no way the police were going to let him walk away with me. There was also nothing stopping him from killing me and then himself in a crazy bid to be together.

"Thomas, the police-"

"Are going to either let both of us go, or neither of us," he said, confirming my thoughts.

Just then, Xander was standing, staring at us, blood dripping down the side of his head. It shocked me that he was able to stand, but I did notice he swayed a bit coming to his feet. This was all my fault. I should have just listened to him, but instead, I let my fear take over and now we were right back where we started, with Thomas having the upper hand.

"I'm sorry," I wept. "I'm so sorry, Xander."

"Police!" Xander turned towards the front door while Thomas just chuckled.

"In here!" Xander answered before turning back to face me and Thomas. "He's got a gun!"

"I also got the girl," Thomas quipped and there was no uncertainty to his mental state anymore. He had to be crazy for none of this to faze him and had there been even a remote chance of confusion, his next words cemented it. "Come on in!" he yelled for the police.

And they did.

The front door crashed open, and four police officers filed in. They immediately took in the scene and every gun was raised and aimed at me and Thomas. Thomas was going to get us killed and maybe that was his plan now. He was going to stay true to his word that if he couldn't have me, then no one could.

"Put the gun down, now!" one of the officers instructed as Xander stood with his hands up, worry lining every inch of his face.

"Or else what, Officer?" Thomas asked, goading him with his insolence. "Are you going to shoot us?"

The cop's eyes darted towards mine as the other three police officers fanned out. "If we have to," he said as calmly as could be, as if my life weren't in danger.

"Sir, come with me," one of the officers said, reaching for Xander.

"No," he barked. "Not without her."

"Don't make me arrest you," she threatened. "Besides, the best thing you can do for her is to go outside with me."

The madness was evident in every word coming out of Thomas's mouth. "Yeah, Xander," he chuckled darkly. "Why don't you go on outside with the nice officer, where it's nice and safe, and leave Fallon here to me."

"You motherfuc-"

"Now!" the officer yelled. "You either leave with me now, or I *will* arrest you for impeding a police matter!"

"Xander, go," I begged. "Please, please go. I'll be okay."

The playfulness was gone when Thomas spoke again. "I'll shoot her where she stands if you don't leave, Xander," he threatened.

I'd never seen such agony on one person's face ever in my life. Xander looked torn. I knew he didn't care about getting arrested, but Thomas's threat to shoot me was real, and Xander knew it. He was going to have to walk out of his house in a small bid to save my life.

"I love you, Fallon," he said, misery in each word. "I fucking love you." Tears streamed down my face as the office escorted him out of the house.

The second that the door closed, the point officer got back down to business. "I need you to put the gun down, sir," he tried again. "Everyone can still walk out of here alive."

Thomas got back to chuckling. "You think I give a shit about that?" He had no concern for the cops on either side of us, guns pointed at our heads.

His attention was on the point officer who, like the others, had his gun pointed as us, too.

"What do you give a shit about?" he asked, trying to negotiate, but even he had to see we were beyond a mutual ending here.

"If I can't have her, no one can," Thomas replied, making it clear the reason we were all here.

"I need you to put the gun down," the cop repeated. "We can't let you hurt her."

Thomas didn't comment, nor did he put the gun down. It was still held to the side of my head and the wait was excruciating. The wait of the unknown was a debilitating thing. Everything was a nightmare that my mind didn't want to process. I was also still disgusted that a tiny part of me didn't want to witness Thomas's death.

Suddenly, I felt Thomas let go of my arm. The gun was still pressed up against my head, but he had released his grip on my arm. I couldn't help it, I turned to face him to try to get a hint as to what he was going to do, but his face was nothing but calm. He was giving nothing away and I didn't know what I was supposed to do now. Run? Fall?

"It's me or it's no one," he repeated in a voice clear and concise for all the room to hear. "That's the only way this ends." Tears started streaming down my face. "They can kill me, Fallon. Hell, they most likely will. But not before I take you with me. You were never meant to be with anyone else. It was always going to be you and me."

Thomas cocked the gun in his hand, and I couldn't stop the cry that escaped. "No!"

And then there was nothing but gunfire.

CHAPTER 24

Xander ~

I dropped to my knees at the sound of gunfire.

This was not supposed to be real-life. This wasn't supposed to be what happened outside action movies. The guilt that I hadn't believed Fallon at first was paralyzing. It's what brought me to my knees. Anyone else might be rushing inside the house to save the woman they loved, but the guilt of not believing her at first had me weakened.

Unwilling to face a life without Fallon was what also had me on my knees on the street. When I had walked out of the house, the officer had forced me to stand behind the patrol cars or face being handcuffed in one of the backseats. I had chosen to behave, all the while, I felt like my emotions were trying to crawl out from beneath my skin.

And as if the guilt weren't enough, everything that made me a man accused me of cowardice. How could I fucking leave her in there? How could I walk out alive to wait? It didn't matter that there were people inside with her that were more qualified to protect her. It didn't matter that they had threatened to arrest me. It didn't matter that I knew my presence might do more harm than good.

None of that mattered.

At the end of the day, I left her to deal with a horrible situation alone. Fuck the cops. Fallon was just a job to them. I was the one who should have protected her better.

I was the one who had failed.

I just prayed to God that she was alive, so that I could make it up to her. I'll spend the rest of my life trailing after her, begging for forgiveness, if that's what I had to do.

As I was bargaining with God, one of the officers came walking out of the house and I didn't care anymore. They could arrest me or fucking shoot me; I needed to get to Fallon.

"Sir!"

I ignored the officer who had escorted me out and raced towards the house. *"Fallon!"*

"Sir!" Now, it was the officer who was walking out of the house that was shouting at me. He had both his hands flat up against my chest, trying to stop me from entering the house.

"Fallon!"

"Sir, you need to-"

"Xander!"

The sound of her voice was all I needed to hear. I stopped fighting and dropped my head back as I thanked God that she was alive. When I opened my eyes and looked beyond the officer who was trying to hold me back, I saw another officer walking out with Fallon in his arms.

She was covered in smeared blood.

I ran towards her, and as soon as I was able, I reached out and yanked her to me. I wrapped my arms around her, not giving two fucks about the blood. "Fallon," I whispered like a prayer. "Oh, baby."

She was shaking, but she was holding on to me just as tightly and I knew there was going to be a long road to recovery, mentally and emotionally. "Xander," she sobbed. "Oh, Xander, they…they…"

I had a fairly good idea of that they had done without her having to explain. I knew the blood wasn't hers, and with the last officer walking out of the house, they were all accounted for. The distant sound of an ambulance told me that I wasn't going to have much time with her and that sent me into a panic.

"Sir, I'm going to have to ask you to step back," the officer who seemed to be in charge said. "Your house is an official crime scene and I need you to follow me out onto the street." I nodded but didn't care. All that mattered was that Fallon was now safe on two fronts. Thomas was dead. He could no longer stalker her, and he no longer had a gun to her head.

With Fallon in my arms, we walked over to the patrol cars just as the ambulance pulled up to the scene. The one female officer immediately went to pull Fallon from my arms, but I held tight. The panic of letting her go was consuming me. "No," I snapped.

The officer narrowed her bright blue eyes at me. "You don't get to tell me no," she snapped back. "If you care *at all* about this woman you will let the paramedics check her out." Then she went for the jugular. "You're going to have to put whatever macho bullshit you're going through aside and do what's best for *her.*"

Before I could comment, Fallon looked up at me. "It's okay, Xander," she whispered. "I…please…"

My fucking heart was breaking.

How the fuck did she expect me to step back yet again? Why was everyone acting like I wasn't the best thing for her right now?

"Fallon-"

She looked at the officer and asked, "Can you question him next to the ambulance?"

Her narrowed blue eyes softened. "Of course," she replied. "But only if you promise to cooperate with the paramedics and not interrupt our preliminary questioning." She reached out and rubbed Fallon's arm. "Once you're medically cleared, you will both have to come down to the station for official questioning."

"That's fine," I agreed.

One of the paramedics walked over, and I was forced to let Fallon go. I watched as he supported her all the way back to the ambulance and I wanted to break something. Everyone else was doing *my* fucking job.

I was graciously allowed to stand on the side of the ambulance as the female officer waited for the officer in charge to join us. Once he did, introductions were made. "Hello," he started, "I'm Officer Nelson and this is Officer Brentwood. What is your name, sir?"

"Xander Raynes," I answered.

"And this is your house?" he asked as both he and Officer Brentwood scribbled on their miniature notepads.

"Yes," I answered.

"And the victim is your wife?"

His question felt like a weight in the pit of my stomach. I was going to have to answer truthfully, and that answer was going to close off all kinds of access to Fallon that I'd normally have as her husband. "No," I replied honestly. "She's my girlfriend, but we live together." I prayed these were the type of people who understood that a legal piece of paper didn't place an exact value on love.

"Her name?"

"Fallon Reese."

"And the man in your home?" He didn't say deceased, so I wondered if it were possible that Thomas could still be alive.

"Uhm, I just know his name is Thomas." I shook my head. "I don't know his last name, only that he and Fallon grew up in foster care together."

Officer Brentwood finally spoke up. "Can you tell us what happened here, Mr. Raynes?"

I ran my hands through my hair and let out a deep breath. They were going to get more details out of Fallon later, so I gave them quick, condensed version of what had happened.

When I was finished, Officer Nelson said, "We'll need you to come down to the station for further questioning."

"What happened in there?" I finally asked.

Officer Brentwood glanced over at Officer Nelson and let him take over again. "If Ms. Reese wants to share the details with you, she may. However, all I can tell you at this time is that we had to use deadly force to resolve the issue at hand." His head jerked towards the back of the ambulance, and I turned to see one of the paramedics giving him a head nod.

I stood there feeling like a fool as Officer Nelson walked over to speak to the paramedic. Officer Brentwood didn't offer anything to fill the silence, and soon, Officer Nelson was walking back towards us. "They're taking her to the hospital for a full checkup. More for her emotional and mental state," he said. "And, well, as much as I hate to do this to you, you're not her husband. We'll need you to come down to the station to give your full statement, and then you can meet her at the hospital."

I wanted to argue.

I wanted to rant and rave, even knowing that I'd get arrested. Still, as I looked around, I finally noticed how the neighbors had gathered around and how a couple of the other officers were taping off my house. I also noticed that some phones were out, and as much as it pained me, I refused to turn Fallon's ordeal into a social media circus. I imagine the paramedics felt the same way because they didn't even give me a chance to talk to her and tell her that I'd see her later. I heard the back of the ambulance doors slam shut and watched as one of the paramedics walked around the side and got into the driver's seat.

I looked over at Officer Nelson and asked, "Can I take my truck or…"

"Do you have your keys with you?"

He had to know I didn't with the way I was half-dressed. "No."

"Then you have to come with us, Mr. Raynes."

That's what I was afraid of.

Well…one of the many things I was afraid of.

CHAPTER 25

Fallon ~

It was dark outside when I finally opened my eyes. The blinds on the window were opened and the night's only light was the moon shining bright.

I glanced around in search of a clock and found one directly in front of the bed. It read 7:13 pm. I'd been asleep for hours. Or, more to the point, I've been passed out for hours.

After the initial inspection of my body and any possible injuries, it was clear that it was my mental and emotional state that were damaged, not my physical wellbeing. However, even after it'd been confirmed that I hadn't suffered any physical harm, I'd had to still sit, covered in Thomas's blood, while they'd taken pictures as evidence. After countless photos, they had finally allowed me to shower before a counselor had appeared in my hospital room.

All the people, tests, questions…through it all, I had just wanted Xander.

I still had to talk to the police in detail about what happened because the hospital counselor had made it clear that I was in no state to speak with them just yet. I had been in shock and probably still was.

When Thomas had cocked his gun, I'd been certain it had meant my death. I knew, without a doubt, that he had truly intended to kill me. I'd also been acceptant of my death. What I hadn't expected was for one of the police officers to take his distraction as an opening to shoot him in the head. Logically, I knew why it had to be a kill shot, but seeing Thomas shot in the head was something that would haunt me forever. I was damaged beyond what was repairable, but even knowing that fact, I still knew I had to try.

I heard the door creak open, and when I looked over, I saw Xander walking into my hospital room, and I'd never been so happy to see someone in my life. "Xander."

I struggled to sit up as he made his way over to the bed. "Goddamn it, Fallon," he swore. "Baby, I've been dying without you."

The tears started and they went on forever. I didn't know how to stop them. The adrenaline crash was real and brutal. I couldn't get a handle on my emotions, and I was terrified Xander would think I wasn't worth the nightmare that had taken place in his home.

"I'm s…sorry, Xand…Xander," I wept. "I'm so, so sorry."

"Hey." I felt him crawl into the bed with me, then gather me up in his arms. Neither of us cared about the wires or monitors. "Baby, you have nothing to be sorry for. God, Fallon," he breathed, "if anything, I'm the one who should be sorry."

I didn't want to go back and forth with the guilt. This wasn't a contest. After a few moments of silence, I asked, "Have you been here the entire time?"

"No," he replied, his lips kissing my hair. "I had to go down to the police station and answer their questions. Give them my statement. Since, uh, we're not married, I wasn't given the choice. But believe me, Fallon, had I had the choice, I would have been here with you the entire time." His arms were like steel bands around me. "I thought I lost you, baby."

We were silent for a few moments, just basking in the comfort of each other's arms, being thankful to both be alive. After a while, he finally asked, "What happened in there?"

What could I say? To repeat the story felt false. I could say the words, but they could never convey the emotions felt in those terrifying moments where Thomas almost shot me, and the police killed him. It wasn't all perfectly orchestrated like an action movie. It had been messy and horrifying, and I knew I was going to need months-if not years-of therapy to be able to sleep at night again.

"Thomas…he…he said he was going to kill me," I told him. "He said I was going to be with him or no one, and he didn't care if he was killed as long as I was, too." Xander's arms tightened around my body. "He cocked…uhm, the cocked the gun, and as soon as it sounded, one of the officers shot him in the head." Chills ran down my spine and I knew Xander could feel me trembling. "I don't know how many times he was shot because I collapsed, and then the officers got me out of there."

"Jesus Christ," he swore. "I'm so fucking sorry."

"I just can't believe it," I sobbed. "That's not the boy I grew up with, Xander. How…how could this happen?"

Xander sighed and held me tighter. "No one knows what it is that connects us to someone, Fallon," he replied. "But since I was willing to die for you, I can understand how he was, too."

"I love you," I whispered, and not because I was in shock, but because now I was no longer afraid to put a name to what I was feeling for Xander. Leaving the attic went beyond doing the right thing. I had left the attic because I was in love with Xander.

"Fallon, you've suffered a-"

I pulled away from him and look up at him. "I know what you're thinking, Xander," I said, interrupting him. "That I'm just experiencing the aftermath of my chaotic emotions, but I'm not." He didn't look convinced, so I added, "Why do you think I left the attic, Xander?"

"I know it's probably too soon and everything is such a fucking mess, but, goddamn, Fallon, I love you, too, baby," he replied and everything in me crashed.

I started sobbing and it just didn't stop.

After I finally calmed down, Xander got off the bed and sat down on the chair next to bed. He had a hold of my hand as he said, "While I was waiting to be questioned by the police, I called Trevor and…told him some of what happened. I told him you were in the hospital, and he and Karla were in the visitor waiting room when I got here."

Oh, God. I had forgotten about Karla. "Can I see them?" I didn't see why I couldn't. I wasn't injured beyond my emotional and mental state, and I so wanted to see them.

Xander gave me a small smile. "You can only have two visitors, but I'll see if I can sneak them by. If not, I'll wait outside, so they can see you."

I nodded, and even though I didn't want Xander to leave my sight, I needed Karla. I needed the connection that only she would understand. When she rushed in, Trevor and Xander behind her, I broke down. She immediately put her arms around me. "Oh, Fallon," she cried. "I'm so glad you're going to be okay."

After a couple of moments, I got myself under control again, and she let go to sit down in the chair Xander had been sitting in earlier. "So am I," I told her honestly.

"What happened?" she asked quietly.

I looked at her, and then glanced over at Xander and Trevor. I knew I was going to need to share the details in order to move past what Thomas had done. Holding it all in wasn't going to help anyone.

I took a deep breath and told them everything. When I was finished, Trevor looked pissed while Karla looked heartbroken. But then, she knew Thomas just like I did. He was a stranger to Xander and Trevor, but to me and Karla, he'd been someone. He had been a friend at one time.

"Jesus," Karla breathed out. "I'm…" She slumped back in her chair. "I'm not sure what I should be feeling right now."

I knew exactly what she meant. It felt like I was feeling everything but nothing at the same time. "He sounded like he really believed that it was love," I told her. "I don't think he saw it as stalking. I really think he thought he was…romancing me or something."

Karla reached over and clasped my hand. "Well, it's over now," she said. "There's still a lot of healing to be had, but at least you won't be looking over your shoulder anymore." Her eyes watered. "You can finally work on having a real life, Fallon."

I looked over at Xander, and it wasn't until he sent me a slow wink and tender smile that I was hit with the realization that I had a chance now. A chance to be near my best friend and a chance at a real family. A life where I could love Xander freely and maybe get married and have children one day.

"What do you say?" I asked, addressing Xander. "You willing to help give me that real life?" He mouthed 'I love you' and it was perfect. I was scared, most likely traumatized, but it was perfect.

After Karla and Trevor finally took their leave, I knew it wouldn't be long before the police showed up. It was late, but I didn't think that would deter them. When the doctor had checked in on me again, I had asked him to convey that I'd be happy to speak with the police first thing in the morning, and he had assured me that he'd do what he could to deter them. It wasn't that I wanted to put it off, so much as I was just so damn tired.

The clock was pointing to well past ten at night when Xander asked, "Why don't we take your savings and my savings and put them together. We could get a nice house with what we have."

I looked over at him surprised. He'd been lounging in the chair next to my hospital bed for a while now as we watched television silently, comfortably. "What?"

He looked at me, those golden eyes looking right through me. "I'd never ask you to go back to my house, Fallon. And since I refuse to be without you, that leaves a fresh start." He let out a deep breath. "Truthfully, I'm not sure I could ever live there again, anyway, with what happened to you. It doesn't feel...it won't feel like home anymore."

It was too soon. Not to mention, we were both in a very delicately emotional state. Still, at one point in time, I had been willing to hand over everything I had to this man when he'd been a stranger to me, so handing everything over now was a no-brainer.

"So, you're finally agreeing with Karla's plan?"

His face was all love. "It's a damn good plan, baby."

EPILOGUE

Fallon – (Ten Years Later) ~
As I tripped-and almost lost an eye again-I wondered why the hell I ever thought being a stay-at-home-mom was a grand idea.

Oh, that's right.

I hadn't imagined my children would be little demons destined to drive me insane.

I kept the F-word firmly planted inside my head and didn't share it with the identical six-year-olds playing in the living room, completely oblivious to my near-death experience. However, to be fair, it was hard to feel anything but love for the two little heathens. They looked exactly like their father and that just sort of tripled my love for them.

It had taken a couple of years to put everything that had happened with Thomas behind me and move forward. It hadn't been until I'd sought professional help that I realized I needed healing from a lot of things beyond that fateful day in Xander's living room. There'd been the classic abandonment that most foster care children feel, but also the six years that Thomas had stalked me. Those years had changed me, and I hadn't even realized it until I had embraced my therapy and strived to help myself overcome everything that I needed to in order to lead a somewhat healthy life. Xander had even attended several sessions with me because he had struggled with not saving me that day, no matter how many times I told him that I didn't fault him in any way.

We had lived together for two years, and during that time, he had given me space to grow into the woman I was today. We'd gotten married after those two years, and while Xander still had his construction company, I had gone to school to get a degree in sociology. However, two years into that, I had fallen pregnant with the twins, and it was all family for me after that. I had toyed with the idea of going back to school once the kids got older, but right now, this was the right choice for me.

"Momma?"

I looked over at Cillian. "What, baby?"

"Why are you holding all our toys if we're going to need them later?"

"She always does that," whispered his image, Cormac.

I could feel my left eye twitching, but before I could give in and just have a nice, well-deserved meltdown, Xander was walking through the front door.

He glanced at the boys, and then looked at me. "Hey, baby," he said, all big smiles.

The breath of relief was real. "Hey," I replied, all the love I had for him in that one word.

He looked at the boys. "What are you guys doing to Momma?" My heart melted just a little more at knowing that Xander could read me so well that he picked up my tentative nervous breakdown by the sound of that one word.

Cillian's shoulders lifted and dropped. "Nothing. She's picking up our toys, and we don't know why, Daddy."

Xander glanced over at me, and his brows shot up in a silent question. I sighed. "You were almost made a widow when I tripped over Max the Maniac Truck," I explained.

Xander walked over towards me, and wrapping his arms around me, murmured in my ear, "Max the Maniac Truck is history. No way am I ever losing you."

It took only two seconds before I started laughing and reveled in how Xander always made everything better. I was outnumbered three to one, but Xander was always on my side.

Setting the toys down, I wrapped my arms around him and let him hold me. Sometimes, even all this time later, Xander needed the reassurance just as much as I did.

I leaned back and looked up at him. "How was your day?"

He smiled and those golden eyes threatened the strength in my knees. "Same thing, different day, baby." He placed a quick kiss on my lips. "How was your day?"

We both turned when we heard a very loud and dramatic sigh. "Don't you care how our day was, Daddy?" Cillian asked while Cormac added, "Momma's day was filled doing mom-things, Daddy. Like it is every day."

I really started laughing then. My life was probably going to be filled with calls from teacher and principals for the next twelve years, and there might be some bail money involved later down the road, but I really was blessed. I had a wonderful family and great friends and I'll never forget how, everything I had, I had by the grace of God.

Xander looked back down at me and smiled. "Well, okay, Momma," he chuckled.

And everything really was okay.

The End.

ABOUT THE AUTHOR

M.E. Clayton works full-time and writes as a hobby. She is an avid reader and, with much self-doubt, but more positive feedback and encouragement from her friends and family, she took a chance at writing, and the Seven Deadly Sins Series was born. Writing is a hobby she is now very passionate about. When she's not working, writing, or reading, she is spending time with her family or friends. If you care to learn more, you can read about her by visiting the following:

Smashwords Interview

Bookbub Author Page

Goodreads Author Page

OTHER BOOKS

The Seven Deadly Sins Series *(In Order)*
Catching Avery (Avery & Nicholas)
Chasing Quinn (Quinn & Chase)
Claiming Isabella (Isabella & Julian)
Conquering Kam (Kamala & Kane)
Capturing Happiness

The Enemy Duet *(In Order)*
In Enemy Territory (Fiona & Damien)
On Enemy Ground (Victoria & William)

The Enemy Series *(In Order)*
Facing the Enemy (Ramsey & Emerson)
Engaging the Enemy (Roselyn & Liam)
Battling the Enemy (Deke & Delaney)
Provoking the Enemy (Ava & Ace)
Loving the Enemy
Resurrecting the Enemy (Ramsey Jr. & Lake)

The Buchanan Brothers Series *(In Order)*
If You Could Only See (Mason & Shane)
If You Could Only Imagine (Aiden & Denise)
If You Could Only Feel (Gabriel & Justice)
If You Could Only Believe (Michael & Sophia)
If You Could Only Dream

The How To: Modern-Day Woman's Guide Series *(In Order)*
How to Stay Out of Prison (Lyrical & Nixon)
How to Keep Your Job (Alice & Lincoln)
How to Maintain Your Sanity (Rena & Jackson)

The Holy Trinity Series *(In Order)*
The Holy Ghost (Phoenix & Francesca)
The Son (Ciro & Roberta)
The Father (Luca & Remy)
The Redemption (Nico & Mia)
The Vatican (Francisco Phoenix Benetti & Luca Saveria Fiore)

The Blackstone Prep Academy Duet *(In Order)*
Reflections (Grace & Styx)
Mirrors (London & Sterling)

The Eastwood Series (In Order)
Samson (Samson & Mackenzie)
Ford (Ford & Amelia)
Raiden (Raiden & Charlie)
Duke (Duke & Willow)
Alistair (Alistair & Rory)

The Problem Series (In Order)
The Problem with Fire (Sayer & Monroe)
The Problem with Sports (Nathan & Andrea)
The Problem with Dating (Gideon & Echo)

The Pieces Series (In Order)
Our Broken Pieces (Mystic & Gage)
Our Cracked Pieces (Rowan & Lorcan)
Our Shattered Pieces (Molly & Grayson)

The Holy Trinity Duet (In Order)
The Bishop (Leonardo & Sienna)
The Cardinal (Salvatore & Blake)

The Holy Trinity Next Generation Series (In Order)
Vincent & Cira (Vincent Fiore & Cira Benetti)
Salvatore Jr. & Camilla (Salvatore Benetti Jr. & Camilla Mancini)
Emilio & Bianca (Emilio Benetti & Bianca Mancini)
Angelo & Georgia (Angelo Benetti & Georgia Mancini)
Dante & Malia (Dante Fiore & Malia Benetti)
Mattia & Remo (Mattia Mancini & Remo Vitale)

The Rýkr Duet (In Order)
Avalon (Avalon & Griffin)
Neve (Neve & Easton)

Standalone
Unintentional
Purgatory, Inc.
My Big, Huge Mistake
An Unexpected Life
The Heavier the Chains…
Real Shadows
You Again
Merry Christmas to Me
Dealing with the Devil

Made in the USA
Las Vegas, NV
31 October 2024